Another Land

PATERSONS IN SCOTLAND

David Carlyle

This is a work of fiction. The events and characters described herein are imaginary and are not intended to refer to specific places or living persons. The opinions expressed in this manuscript are solely the opinions of the author and do not represent the opinions or thoughts of the publisher. The author has represented and warranted full ownership and/or legal right to publish all the materials in this book.

Another Land
Patersons in Scotland

v2.0

Outskirts Press, Inc.
http://www.outskirtspress.com

ISBN: 978-1-4787-0339-6

Library of Congress Control Number: 2013910147

PRINTED IN THE UNITED STATES OF AMERICA

Chapter 1

1876 – April 23, 1880

Edna looked around her big room in the McCarty mansion near Inverness, Scotland. She rarely argued with her father, but this morning she penned a plan to do it, because no time remained for calm persuasion. She sat at her desk, dipped a pen into her inkwell, and wrote:

'Monday, August 7, 1876
Quarrel with Father
Stamp foot
Cry
Refuse to go'

She looked briefly at her composition, touched a corner of it to the candle in her room, and dropped it on the stone floor to burn completely. She took a deep breath, squared her shoulders, and walked to the dining hall to meet her father for early breakfast. He waited there for her.

She raised her foot and opened her mouth, but then hesitated, and Arthur, her father, spoke first. "Are you all right, Edna?"

"Yes, Father, I'm all right." She didn't stamp her foot, but hesitated again.

"Your face is flushed. Are you sure you're not sick?"

"Yes, Father, I'm fine." She lowered her foot.

"Sit down and enjoy your breakfast. I want to watch you eat your pancakes here one last time before you go."

Edna sighed and sat. "Very well, Father. I must talk to you, however.

You know I don't want to go, don't expect to survive the trip, and even if I leave an heir, don't expect you to live long enough to meet or protect that heir, if perchance he or she tries to find you."

A clock in a hallway chimed six times. "You're the apple of my eye, Edna, but you speak nonsense. We'll have plenty of time to talk during our ride to Glasgow Port. I told the liveryman to pull up to the south mansion door at exactly 7:00, and the butler to come to your room for your trunk at two minutes till. So we can't waste time now."

Edna and her father ate their breakfast quickly, Edna went back to her room, and closed the door. Someone knocked and called through the door. "Miss Edna? I'm here for the trunk."

"I'm not going today. Please tell my father."

The clock chimed seven times. Someone again knocked and called, "Edna, this is Father. I'll carry your trunk myself. May I come in?"

"Did the butler say anything to you?"

"He said you didn't open the door for him."

Edna sighed again and opened the door. Arthur hoisted the trunk to his shoulder and walked ahead of Edna, out the south mansion door, and to the carriage. He gave the trunk to the liveryman, and held the carriage door for her.

Edna stepped up into the carriage and said, "You know I don't want to go. Will you change your mind?"

Arthur merely shook his head and entered the carriage. The liveryman began the two-day trip to Glasgow Port to meet a ship to New York. Arthur summarized his plan for Edna to board the ship, audit classes for four years at the University of Rochester in New York, and then return. "Your brother Eric studied there, and you deserve the same opportunity he had."

Edna allowed her father to finish. "I don't want to go, but it appears I must. You'll keep an eye on Rex Smalley won't you? I don't trust him for a minute, and I hope you don't either after what he did, and the rumors we heard. I'll feel much better if you allow me to stay with you."

A smile erupted on Arthur's face. "Don't concern yourself about Rex. I understand why you fear him, and I already told you I'll do whatever I must to keep him away from you. That's another reason I want you out of the country for a while, and want him here where I can watch him. He's looked after my estate almost three years, however, and does fine work with the land and shops. He serves at my pleasure, and knows plenty of other people want his job." Arthur took time to fill and light his pipe. "It's normal for people to envy our wealth. They pestered your Grandfather Erroll all the while he built our estate, but he lived a long and happy life. I'll do the same."

"All right, but be careful. I have a secondary reason too, to want to stay here. I'm not sure I can keep pace with the men at the university. I'll be younger than most of them, and will be a foreigner in their land."

"We've discussed your fear many times, Edna. You did well with your private tutors at the mansion, and you'll do fine at the University." He patted her arm.

"Very well, Father. I know you don't know best this time, but I suppose I must honor your wishes. You'll send a letter to me every time you go to Glasgow, won't you?"

"Yes, Edna, every time. You study hard and come back here smart, you hear?" The smile remained on Arthur's face.

Edna abandoned her sad look and giggled. "Yes, Father, I hear. Do you really think I'll come back any other way?"

Edna's ship waited at a dock on the south side of River Clyde when she and Arthur came to the river's north bank. They crossed on a ferry, both went on board the ship, and Edna worried again. "Don't forget to watch out for Rex Smalley. I've not recovered from the loss of Mother, and I don't want to lose you too." After a quiet moment she disclosed a recurring dream. "I see myself leaving Scotland as an adult. And I see myself—or someone—coming back later as a child, but you're not here."

Arthur first laughed, but then responded seriously. "We all dream strange things, Edna. Put it out of your mind, and enjoy the new places you're about to see." They embraced, and he left the vessel. Edna stood by a rail as he waited for the ferry and eventually stepped onto it. She watched Arthur until her ship steamed away from the dock, then went below deck, and stayed there during most of the trip. She disembarked when her ship docked at New York's South Street Seaport, and soon after, boarded a boat to go up the Hudson River/Erie Canal waterway to Rochester.

Arthur prearranged permission for Edna to audit history classes at the University of Rochester before she left Scotland. She didn't register as a regular student there, because the university admitted only men as full students. Arthur sent money ahead to pay for her room and board at a prestigious rooming house nearby, and she hired a coach to take her from the boat to her new home.

Edna studied without incident for a time. She found a church near the school, and met an older man there, named John Paterson. John had reddish sandy hair like hers, looked vigorous and strong like her father, and stood nearly as tall as her father at perhaps barely under six feet. John talked often to her, and asked her several times to go with him to Sunday dinner at his mother's home, where he lived.

Edna rejected John's invitations with a variety of excuses—weather's too hot or too cold, must study, must help roommate—but she eventually agreed to dinner on a blustery December Sunday. John tried to prepare her to meet his mother. "Mom's a really nice person, but she can talk pretty rough sometimes. I'm over twenty-seven years old—maybe I shouldn't tell you this—but Mom ran off the only other girl I introduced to her, and made her cry."

"I hope she likes me, but she won't chase me away, because I accepted an invitation to visit you, not her."

Confident talk notwithstanding, Edna suffered a rocky start with

October of that year. The letter read, 'Sorry to hear of Edna's death. Will you come to supervise my cattle crews west of Inverness?'

John wrote back, 'I appreciate your offer, but have a job here and don't know anything about cattle. I must respectfully decline.'

Letters traveled across the Atlantic slowly in those days, so even though John responded promptly, a reply didn't come until December. 'My people already know about cattle. What you'll do is make sure they stay on the job. I can pay you what you make now—how much is that?—plus 30%. And I'll provide a house, chickens, and a horse for you. Please change your mind.'

John's income didn't cover his expenses, he ran through his savings, mortgaged the house, and depleted the proceeds. He wrote back, 'I'll come. Must wait for warmer weather to travel. I make $12.50 a week.'

In a last letter exchange, John received a pay offer in pounds equivalent to $16.25 a week and he answered with a travel schedule. He would leave Rochester on the Erie Canal Monday, April 4, 1887, leave New York Sunday, and arrive at Glasgow Port Wednesday, April 20, if ship schedules were accurate. He sent the schedule letter, sold the house, rented it back, paid off the mortgage, bought three tickets to Scotland, and enough remained for the family to live for a couple months.

John told Kenzie and Erroll about the upcoming trip before it began. "Hey kids, we made it to Saturday again, so Jo won't come today. We'll be here by ourselves."

The children displayed gap-toothed grins, and Kenzie expressed their feeling. "Yippee!"

John grinned too, then turned more serious. "I need to tell you something. We're about to go on a long trip." Both children grinned wider. "We'll get on a ship here in Rochester on Monday morning, ride on it through places you've never seen, and stop at one of those places called New York City. We'll stay in that city overnight, get on another ship, and travel across the ocean to another land, where I'll work with Uncle Eric's cattle. We won't stay forever, but will come back some day. How does that sound?"

Erroll asked an important question. "Can we steer the ship?"

Kenzie asked another important question before John could answer. "Will Jo come?"

He skipped Erroll's question. "No, Jo will stay behind. Is that all right with you?"

Erroll answered ahead of Kenzie. "Yes, it will be all right. Right, Kenzie?"

"Yep."

Erroll started a new line of questions. "Are Uncle Eric's cattle on a farm?"

"I think they are."

"Will we live on a farm?"

"I think we will."

"Can we go out and play all over the farm whenever we want to?"

"Pretty much. But today we need to gather up what we want to take. We can't take a lot, but we can choose. I'll get the small trunk down from upstairs and put it on your bed. We can put things in it we want to take, but when it's full, we can't take any more."

Kenzie nodded. "We understand."

They selected everything to take, put it in the trunk, and made it ready a day ahead. They included all their clothes, one small toy each for Kenzie and for Erroll, and all 4 of John's books: his Bible, Aileen's recipe book, a history of Rochester, and an accounting textbook. They debated about other items, left most behind, and took nothing but the trunk except for a loaf of bread John asked Kenzie to carry in her hands, the clothes they wore, and John's pocket watch and pocketknife.

Chapter 4

1887

John already had the tickets, and the family walked a fraction under five blocks to get on a ship headed to New York City. They went on board almost an hour before departure, and the children explored every square foot of their new environment. They grew tired of the trip before they arrived in New York City, however, and gladly got off the ship there. They wanted to see everything in the city, but John pointed out they didn't have enough time or money for that, so they found a place to stay the night before they boarded another ship for the Atlantic crossing. They went on the ship about an hour early again, and the children enjoyed checking out the bigger and different ship, but again tired of the trip, and wanted it to end before it did.

John had plenty of time to tell the children about the ocean they traveled on, the sea creatures in it, and even about fishing methods. In turn, the children peppered John with questions. For example, Erroll asked, "Why does Kenzie have a different name than we do?"

John answered almost too quickly, "Kenzie has parents. Her mom went to a place called California when Kenzie could barely walk and talk, and she loved Kenzie too much to take her to that wild place. Her dad went to Kentucky about the same time, and he couldn't take care of her there either."

Kenzie asked a follow up. "Why do I live with you?"

"Because we love you more than anybody else in the world does, and we want you more than anybody else does. You probably don't know it, but when Erroll's mother and I married, I told her I'd love her, comfort and keep her, and remain true to her as long as I had breath. I tell you and Erroll the same thing now. You're everything to me, and I'll work for your good as long as I live. Because of that, I hope to take you back to New York some day."

Much of John's speech apparently flew over Kenzie's head, because she inquired about an earlier statement. "When could I barely walk and talk?"

"About four years ago."

"Where did I come from?"

"From across the street, where your parents lived."

"How did they get me?"

"Your mom gave birth to you."

"How did that happen?"

"Birth is a complicated subject, and you need to be bigger to understand it all. I'll try to explain it when you're a lot older than you are now."

The family woke early on Wednesday, April 20, because the travel schedule stated they'd dock at Port Glasgow that day. They steamed through the Firth of Clyde, a huge body of water similar to more ocean, except they occasionally saw land. They reached the dock in Port Glasgow soon after lunch, and got off the ship. John held the trunk on his shoulder with his left hand, held Kenzie's hand with his right, and Kenzie held Erroll's hand. They tried to find Eric McCarty, but didn't know what he looked like, so they asked around. They eventually crossed to the north side of River Clyde and briefly looked for Eric there, until John put the trunk on the ground at the edge of a street leading north away from the river.

After a long time of waiting, John re-shouldered the trunk and explained to the children, "It's late. Maybe Uncle Eric won't come until tomorrow. He knows our ship arrived today, so I'm sure he won't forget about us. We'll find a place to eat and stay the night, and come back here tomorrow."

They put the trunk down and took turns sitting on it when they returned the next day. They waited for Eric to find them, until a young man in a uniform approached, and spoke to John. "Are ye John Paterson?"

"Yes. Are you Eric McCarty?"

"No, Ah'm 'is liveryman. Ah'm t' take ye back t' th' McCarty estate."

"Great. Let me introduce Erroll and Kenzie to you."

"Never mind. If ye 'ave young'uns with ye, they're your problem and Mr. McCarty's, not ma ain."

John's face flushed slightly. "They're not anybody's problem. But we're all here and we can't afford to go back. We're ready to go if you are. What's your name?"

The liveryman ignored the question. "Fine. Ma carriage's waitin' on th' street. We'll travel 'bout 210 km, and stop for th' night at Glencoe, 'bout 'alfway. Keep th' young'uns quiet."

The young man led, the Paterson family followed, and stepped up into the carriage. The liveryman lifted the trunk to the top, climbed to a seat up front, and the carriage lurched. They traveled only a few seconds before Kenzie asked, "Why doesn't the man like us?"

John speculated, "Maybe he's not as lucky as we are. Maybe he has to live by himself and doesn't know anybody your age. We're his guests now in any case, so we need to do what he says."

"Will Uncle Eric like us?"

John responded with a non-answer. "I don't know, Kenzie. I hope he will and think he will, because his sister, Erroll's mother, liked Erroll and me very much. She loved us. We have to wait and see about Uncle Eric."

The carriage bounced and swayed all day. The driver stopped near some brushy areas for a couple bathroom breaks, but didn't stop for a meal until almost dark. The children begged for food from before noon until they stopped to eat and sleep at a tavern in Glencoe. The liveryman told John, "Mr. McCarty gave me money t' pay for your meal, but 'e didn't send money for no young'uns."

John's face flushed again. "Keep your money. I'll pay for the children's food as well as mine." The children ate ravenously, as did John.

John asked during the meal, "Do you know what work Eric wants me to do?"

"Ah never talk 'bout Mr. McCarty's bi'ness."

He tried again. "Do you know where we'll live?"

"Ah already telt ye. Ah never talk 'bout Mr. McCarty's bi'ness. If ye wanta stay alive, ye won't ask no more questions."

John used most of his remaining money to pay for breakfast the next morning, and to buy food to stash in his pockets for the children later in the day.

The group boarded the carriage after breakfast, endured another long bumpy day of riding, traveled through part of Inverness, and turned west. The road west out of Inverness initially skirted water—a big body of it—to the north, diverged from the water, continued past a huge mansion on the north, and past a wooded area on the south. The liveryman turned left off the road and went nearly a half mile up a slope on grass—no road, only a footpath—shortly after he drove by the wooded area, and stopped the carriage in front of an unpainted little wood shack, about fourteen feet by fourteen feet, with a small shed on the west side. The shack had a gable roof, towered over by roughly a quarter-acre of the tallest weeds John had seen in Scotland. He saw no windows and only one door, but noticed a stack of sticks and twigs near the door on the left.

The liveryman climbed down from his seat at the front of the carriage, came back, opened the door, and ordered, "Git out. Ye gonna set there all night? This 'ere's it."

John inquired, "This is what?"

"I telt ye t' stop askin' questions. This 'ere's where ye live. The McCarty mansion's back yonder." The liveryman pointed northeast at the hidden-by-trees mansion they saw from the carriage a few minutes earlier.

“We can’t stay here. Hogs live in better places than this back in New York.”

“Ye ain’t in New York. This ‘s where ye live. Don’t make no waves. Chust go in ‘nd shut up.”

“We won’t stay here. Take us back to the mansion and we’ll stay with Eric tonight.”

The liveryman’s face paled noticeably, even in the dusky light. “I ain’t gonna do ‘t. Mr. McCarty telt me t’ bring ye ‘ere. Ah never question Mr. McCarty’s orders.”

“Then we’ll walk. Take our trunk back there please.”

“Ye don’t wanta go there Mr. Paterson, take ma word for ‘t.”

“We do want to go there, because we won’t stay in a shack like this.”

“Ah don’t wanta scare ye, but if ye care about your ain life or these ‘ere young’uns’, ye’ll chust go in and shut up. I beg ye Mr. Paterson, chust do ‘t.”

“Do you know something we don’t?”

“Please, Mr. Paterson, chust do ‘t.”

“Well . . . whatever you think. Thanks for your advice. Will we find food inside?”

“Don’t thank me for that. Ah chust done what Mr. McCarty telt me t’ do. Ye’ll someday th—never mind. ‘Bout food, th’ place’s been empty a couple o’ weeks. There’s prob’ly eggs in th’ chicken ‘ouse.”

Chapter 5

1887

"All right. Be careful going back to wherever it is you go." The liveryman didn't answer. He unloaded the trunk, put it on the dirt path in front of the shack door, climbed up on the front of the carriage, went back across the grass to the road, and turned toward Inverness and the mansion.

Kenzie implored with a distressed tone, "Don't we have food?"

Erroll followed, "We gotta have food."

John might have been distressed too, but he tried to calm the children. "We'll find something. Let's try to go inside and see what's in there." He pushed the door and it opened easily. They went in, but their eyes required a few minutes to adjust. John found a place on the floor to set the trunk, but they didn't see much in the partial darkness. They first saw a narrow bed against the south wall in the east corner, and a table near the middle of the one room, supporting an empty bucket, a food-encrusted plate, knife, fork and cup. The shack didn't have windows or a stove for heating or cooking.

They saw a series of hooks on the east wall when their eyes adjusted more. The hooks supported a roughly one-quart container with cup handle, a skillet, two pots, medium and small, and a dishpan. They continued to look, and found a short shelf in the northeast corner holding salt and pepper in shakers, a large box of matches, a box of rifle shells, and an open coffee can with flour in it. Mouse droppings covered the surface of the flour, so John took the can to the door and dumped the flour on the grass.

They discovered a scythe, a medium tub, shovel, broom, rifle, and a thick board about 4 feet long in the northwest corner of the shack.

Wood boards covered the floor, with few cracks between. Kenzie checked out the bed. It had a board bottom—no springs—with a thin mattress on it covered by a blanket.

Erroll begged again. "We gotta have food."

John answered Erroll's plea a second time. "The liveryman said eggs might be in the chicken house. Let's look." They went outside to search for a chicken house, and eventually discovered chickens in the little shed on the side of the larger shack, so John bent down, went in, and called to the children outside. "I found eggs, lots of eggs. I'll come out and get the dishpan to put them in."

When John emerged from the shed for the dishpan, Kenzie asked, "How will you cook eggs without a stove?"

"I'll get the eggs and then we'll think of something." He went back in the chicken house and brought out nineteen eggs. "I saw matches inside. We'll use those to build a fire outside, and then we'll use the skillet to fry eggs." He built the fire but couldn't find grease; he told Kenzie he could scramble eggs in a greaseless skillet better than he could fry them.

John held the skillet in the fire and broke a rotten egg into it. He scraped out the skillet as well as he could with a small stick and broke another egg, not rotten this time. He allowed the children to share eggs until they were full, then he ate a couple. The skinny little five-year-old children ate a total of seven eggs before John had one. Even after he threw out a few more rotten ones, however, he eventually filled everybody, and several eggs remained.

Erroll proclaimed another problem. "I'm thirsty."

Kenzie followed, "Me too."

John didn't know how or what they'd drink, but suggested they poke around in the weeds to look for a pump. They didn't find one, but continued to look until they found a stream at the edge of a woods they would later hear called Big Wood, about thirty yards east of their shack. The children fell on their stomachs to drink directly from the stream. John wondered if he should try to stop them, because he didn't know what might be in the water, but he didn't want to wait either, so he crouched down and followed their example.

He announced the children's bedtime after they all had a drink, but Erroll mentioned yet another problem. "I have to go to the bathroom."

Kenzie followed again, "Me too."

John proposed they separately hide in the weeds west of the shack and make do without a formal bathroom, because he couldn't think of anything better. He looked at the bed before the children came back from the weed patch, and found the mattress filthy, the same as everything else in the shack. He put the mattress out on the grass in front of the shack, and swept the floor. The children returned before he completed the floor work, but he finished and gave sleeping instructions. "We'll all sleep on the floor tonight. We won't need pajamas, but I'll open the trunk, because you might like to sleep with your jacket over your clothes. I'll wash the mattress tomorrow, and Kenzie, you can sleep on the bed after tonight. I think I'll hang the blanket across the corner where the bed is, to give you privacy behind it."

He helped the children find a place on the floor, and pulled his winter coat from the trunk to cover them both. They soon fell asleep, because they were up early that day. He took the bucket outside by the fire, along with all cooking utensils except the dishpan with eggs in it. He put more wood on the fire, took the bucket to the stream for water, set the bucket in the fire, left it there until the water boiled, and scalded all the food-contact items. He went to the stream for one more bucket of water, boiled it, and set it on the table inside the shack to cool. Then he put out the fire and found a spot on the floor. He didn't bother to look at his watch, but fell asleep quickly.

John scrambled more eggs for Sunday breakfast, and put the bucket back in the fire to heat water to wash the mattress. A hatless man with a dour face rode up to the shack on a horse, while John waited for the water to boil. The rider asked, "You John Paterson?"

"Yes, and I suppose you're Eric?"

The person peered down a haughty nose at John and snarled, "That would be Mister McCarty to you."

"Whatever you say, Mister McCarty." He called to the children in the shack. "Come on out kids, and meet Uncle Er—meet Mister McCarty."

Kenzie led the way. "Hi, Uncle Eric."

Erroll followed. "Hey, Uncle Eric, I bet you don't know where we slept last night."

The horseman ignored the children and addressed John. "I'm here to tell you what to do. I don't have a lot of time."

John adopted the time-is-short view. "Fine. Shoot."

"You'll check on the cattle crews seven days a week, 365 days a year, starting tomorrow. Walk up to the stable, check out a horse from the stable boy, ride west, and find three herds. You'll find'em if you leave the road and go mainly west and a little south, the closest just over yonder hill, the farthest about twelve km out, past Hummer Wood. You want to find three herdsmen with each herd, but they quit at the drop of a hat. They're scum. They continually try to cheat me, and as my representative, they'll do the same to you. Be sure they're on the job, and if you don't see three, ask where the missing one or two are. If they've quit, then go into Inverness when you get back and hire the needed number, which'll be easy, because loafers hang around on public streets. You'll find'em, and when you hire, tell'em I'll pay the equivalent of $5.00 a week when I get around to it."

"Back to the crews—each group has a rifle with one or two shells they use to shoot game. They'll want more shells, but make them account for the two they had before. Don't give them too many, lest we have an armed insurrection on our hands; take shells with you, but only a few, so you don't become a robbery target. Pick up shells and also matches at the stable and take both with you, but give them out sparingly. Be sure you have the horse back at the stable before dark, don't ride the horse for any purpose except to check on the crews, and don't let a herdsman on a horse, ever."

"Yes, Sir, Mr. McCarty." John paused. "Is there a school around here for Erroll and Kenzie? May they stay at the mansion with you during the day while I'm at work?"

The boss glared. "I didn't know you'd bring kids with you, but since you did, it's up to you to keep them out of my business and away from your work."

He turned his horse and rode back down the path; Kenzie pointed with obvious disbelief. "He's not Uncle Eric, is he?"

John answered, "He says he is. He isn't like we want, but we can't worry about him, because we have lots of work to do. Today might be the last available for a while."

John washed the mattress, but couldn't find a good place to dry it when he finished. After he tried a few places that didn't work, he draped the mattress over some approximately horizontal tree limbs down by the stream. He dug his and her latrines, and used the scythe to mow weeds around the shack, but left a couple C-shaped weed enclosures around the latrines. The children preferred to take their baths in the stream rather than at the shack, so John allowed them to do it rather than carry water for them. He fixed a broken door on the chicken house, so he could close it after the chickens came in for the night and open it after sunup, when chicken predators would be less active. He filled an empty waterer in the chicken house and counted; he found two roosters and eight hens, plus two more hens with thirteen nearly half-grown chicks. He hung the bedspread as he intended, shot and cooked a squirrel for lunch, saved three pieces for supper, and saved a tiny amount of grease to use with eggs.

He checked on the mattress and found it not yet dry, so Kenzie slept on the floor a second night.

Chapter 6

1887

John awakened the children early Monday for a standard breakfast of scrambled eggs, and gave them rules to follow after he rode away on the horse. "Rule one is never let anyone inside the shack unless you know them and feel safe with them. Use the board in the corner to bar the door if you're not sure about someone, and then remain quiet and don't let anyone know you're in here. For rule two, stay close to the shack and don't go near the stream or into the woods when I'm gone. Finally, don't try to cook, no matter how hungry you may be. I'll probably return late for lunch every day, but will know you're hungry and will get back here as soon as I can. Do you understand all that, and why I say it?"

Erroll answered, "Yes."

Kenzie added, "Me too."

John walked toward the stable immediately and soon rode past on a horse. The children stood in front of the shack and waved, so John waved back, but didn't slow. He came to the first herd just over the hill closest to the shack, and found the three herdsmen in a group. John went near them, dismounted, and tied the horse to a tree. "Hello."

The men muttered among themselves, but after a while, one called out, "Hello."

He approached the speaker. "I'm John Paterson, representing Mr. McCarty. What's your name?"

The speaker looked away and then down, but eventually answered. "Ah'm Ron Everett."

John inquired, "And who are your friends?"

Ron remained reticent, but after John asked again, he pointed and named them, "This's Bob and that's Orville."

As a step to put a regular business relationship in place of the master/scum hierarchy his boss described, John asked, "Who's in charge here?"

Ron replied, "Nobody's in charge. Maybe ye."

"No, I mean when I'm not around."

Ron said, "Nobody."

John tried again. "Will you choose somebody now?"

"Choose somebody?"

"Yes, will the three of you decide who your leader is?"

"Why do we need a leader?"

"A leader can represent you to me, can make decisions, and will be good for you, for the cattle, and for me. Will you choose one?"

The other two men pointed at Ron. Before he could protest, John confirmed, "Great. Is everything going along here like you want it to go?"

"Ah suppose."

"Do you need anything?"

"No."

John backed away toward his horse. "I'll go on to the other two herds. I don't plan to stop when I come back by here, but if you think of anything, put both your hands up when you see me, like this," John demonstrated, "and I'll stop. Bye Ron. Bye Bob. Bye Orville."

John mounted his horse, waved, and rode on west. Ron waved back immediately, and after a delay, both Bob and Orville nodded. John conducted similar conversations with people at the other two herds. He tried to connect with the herdsmen in each crew, but didn't stay long anywhere.

He returned to the shack in the early afternoon, stopped, and tied the horse to a tree behind the shack, out of sight of the road. He explained to the children he didn't want his boss to discover he returned to the stable early and perhaps think the job too easy, or to ride by and see him cooking before he returned the horse to the stable.

John told Erroll and Kenzie to carry wood from the front of the shack to the back, where he built a fire and scrambled more eggs. Kenzie complained. "All we ever eat here is scrambled eggs. Can't we have something else?"

Erroll agreed. "Wouldn't it be great if we had tomato soup and ham?"

John counseled patience. "I'll take the horse back to the stable and walk into Inverness after we eat. I'll buy flour to make gravy, and lard so we can cook eggs in different ways. I'll also look for garden seeds. We'll find another squirrel tomorrow, and our little chickens will be big enough we can have fried chicken in a few weeks. We'll eat fried chicken and things from the garden before summer ends."

Erroll did a somersault and hopped a couple times. "That sounds great, Poppa! I can't hardly wait!"

Kenzie skipped the acrobatics, but agreed. "I hated garden stuff in Rochester, but now that I'm here, I really want it. Can you get seeds for green beans and tomatoes?"

"I don't know what's for sale here. I'll get those if they have them, but we'll need to wait for them to grow. I must go away for a little while again to buy that stuff, even though I don't want to go. I worried about you when I left you here this morning, but must do it every day. How'd you do while I was gone today?"

Kenzie answered, "Fine."

Erroll modified Kenzie's answer. "We didn't do real bad, but Kenzie got scared."

"What scared you Kenzie?"

"Nothing, I just practiced." She grinned.

"What did you practice?"

Erroll broke in, "She practiced barring the door."

"That's a relief, and isn't wrong, Erroll. Practice is always good."

"But she wouldn't let me in."

"Is that right Kenzie? Did you bar the door with Erroll outside?"

"Yes." She grinned again.

"Let's all go in and practice again. We never want to put up the bar when one of us is outside. Never."

They all went in the shack, John asked Kenzie to show how she barred the door, and then asked Erroll to do it. He reiterated the purpose of the bar is to lock out potential intruders, not family members. Then he took the horse back to the stable and walked to Inverness.

He came back from Inverness with everything he went for, and said he also saw a nice thick rug they could sleep on, but didn't have enough money to buy it; "I did buy seeds, however. I bought tomato seeds. We can put dirt inside eggshells and start the tomatoes in those. I found green beans, peas, navy beans, and cucumbers we can plant outside. We can look forward to potatoes this evening and more later, because I bought a pound of them. I'll cook three potatoes tonight and we'll plant the rest. It's late for potatoes but they might work. Do you remember how we plant them?"

Erroll did. "Yep. We cut 'em in pieces and stick 'em in dirt, same as we did in Rochester. We had more to eat when we lived there. Can we go back there?"

"No, we don't have any money, but we'll eventually eat better here too. Who wants to go out and help plant potatoes?"

The children said they wanted to go. John cut the potatoes with his pocketknife and dug little holes with the shovel, while Kenzie dropped chunks in the holes and Erroll raked dirt over them with his hands. John helped the children plant the other seeds too, and gave them more work to do later. "The chickens will want to eat our little plants when they poke out of the ground. Your job is to let them out of their shed in the mornings, and then shoo them away when they come near our garden. Can you do that?"

Erroll asserted, "Yep. We can do it."

Kenzie objected, "We can try, but there are a lot more chickens than there are Erroll and me."

"Just do the best you can. The chickens are our friends. They won't know they're doing wrong when they try to eat our garden, so the garden will be yours to protect and theirs to eat. You probably won't win every time, but stop them as often as you can."

Erroll stuck out his boyish chest. "Yes we *will* win every time. Chickens are afraid of people. We'll never let them in the garden."

John smiled. "Just do your best. I can't ask you for more than that." He waited a moment and talked about the next morning. "I don't like to leave you here by yourselves for even a minute, but it might work better if I get up early, scramble a couple eggs to leave on the table, and go to work while you're still asleep. Maybe I'll get back by noon. Does that sound all right to you?"

Kenzie answered and included a complaint. "We're fine by ourselves, but I really don't like scrambled eggs."

"Scrambled eggs are all we have for breakfast, and it might be that way for a while. If I'm gone when you wake up, look on the table for breakfast. I'll come back as soon as I can. All right?"

Erroll said, "All right," but Kenzie didn't answer.

John didn't awaken as early the next morning as he hoped, but the children continued to sleep, so he built a fire outside and scrambled three eggs. He ate one, left the others in separate pots on the table, grabbed the quart cup off its hook, closed the shack door quietly, and walked to the stable to get his horse for the day. He knew where to go on Tuesday, and thus made better time. He came to the first herd, dismounted a short distance away, and walked to the three men as before.

He spoke to newly elected leader Ron. "Is everything all right with you three today?"

"Yeah. We're fine."

"Are the cattle all right today?"

"Yeah, they're fine."

"Does this herd have a name?"

"A name?"

"Yes. There are three herds on the estate. Maybe they'll be easier to talk about if each has a name."

"This 'erd don't 'ave no name."

"Will you talk to Bob and Orville and invent one by tomorrow?"

"If that's what ye want."

"I don't talk to the boss every day, but when I do, it'll be nice to tell about the herds by name."

Ron broke eye contact with John. "McCarty don't know ma name. Why do ye think 'e'll remember a 'erd's name?"

"I don't know why the boss doesn't know your name, but the next time I talk with him I'll tell him your name, and Bob's and Orville's, along with the names of his other six herdsmen. And I'll tell him the names of his herds if they have them. Will you tell me a name tomorrow?"

Ron looked at Bob and Orville, but they didn't look back. After a moment of indecision, Ron said, "Yeah, Ah think we can 'ave a name tomorrow."

John smiled and shook hands with all three herdsmen. "There's one other thing. I have this cup here," he held up the cup, "and want to fill it with milk if there's a cow that will let me. Do you know one that might?"

Ron pointed, "That tall one over there. She lost 'er calf. Me and Bob and Orville drink 'er milk ever' day."

"Thanks, I'll remember that. I need to see the people at the other two herds this morning, but I'll be back today and will fill my cup. Thanks again." John shook everybody's hand again, went back to his horse, and continued west.

He visited each of the other crews that morning, and asked each to give him a herd name on Wednesday. He encountered no problems at the second herd, but saw only two people with the third herd. Leader Art explained Stan sometimes had an upset stomach, and he did that day. "Stan's been sick three times since he started work here. I'll fire him if you want me to."

John held up his right hand and emphasized, "Oh no, don't fire him. Can you and Thomas take care of the herd while Stan rests?"

"Oh yes, I can do it myself. We don't do that much."

"You and Thomas do it then, and we won't fire Stan. He needs to know we want him here and his job is secure."

"Did you run that past McCarty?"

"I don't see the boss every day, but if Stan can't work here, then I can't work here either. Where is Stan?"

"He's on his back in the shack." Art pointed and John looked.

The woods partly hid a shack like the one he lived in, right down to the chicken house on the side. He walked over to talk to Stan. "Hi Stan, I rode through here yesterday. Do you remember me?"

"Aye."

"How you feeling?"

"Not good, but Ah should be better any minute now, and'll get back t' work."

"Take your time. Art said he and Thomas can handle the cattle indefinitely, and your job will be here when you're able to come back to it."

"Aye, right." Stan's tone exuded disbelief.

"Really. Don't go back to work until you feel up to it. The boss will never hear you're sick."

"Aye, right."

"Art vouched for you, and your job is safe as long as you have Art in your corner. Nobody except Art will fire you for being sick, and if Art does it, he'll need to explain why to me."

"I hope ye're tellin' the truth Mr. uh—"

"Paterson. John. And I am."

"Thanks."

"Just rest here until you feel better. Bye." John went back east, past herd two. He looked for a shack as he rode by the herd and saw it, also partly hidden behind a grove of trees. He milked the tall cow at the first herd and talked again to the herdsmen. He didn't mention a name but Ron reported they already had one.

John asked, "What is it?"

"Beauty Firth Beauties, after yon Beauty Firth." Ron gestured toward Beauty Firth, down the hill north.

"That's a great name, Ron. Magnificent. Thank you."

"It was Orville's idea."

"Thanks, Orville. And thank you all for agreeing to it so quickly. That name shows you have pride in your herd."

Bob responded to the 'your herd' notion. "It ain't our herd. It's McCarty's."

"Yes, but the cattle are yours to care for, and I know they do better because you're proud of them."

Bob said, "Maybe. Whatever you think. Bye."

John went back to his horse. He mounted carefully to avoid spilling milk, saw the first group's shack, went on past it, and came to his shack a few minutes before noon. He found Erroll and Kenzie sitting on the ground by the garden, and again tied the horse behind the shack. The children came around back, and John saw tear streaks down Erroll's dirty face. "Did you cry while I was gone today, Erroll?"

"Maybe."

"Why?"

Erroll didn't answer, so John asked Kenzie. "Do you know why Erroll cried today?"

She shrugged and went around to the front of the shack, so John tried one more time. "What happened to make you cry, Erroll?"

"Kenzie did it."

"What did Kenzie do?"

"She called me a wicked step-brother."

"I see. You're not wicked are you?"

"No."

"You're not a step-brother either, so you can forget about it, all right? I brought milk today. Go find Kenzie and tell her about it."

Erroll went around the shack and brought Kenzie back. John held up the cup, mentioned the milk inside, and promised, "We can have real gravy for lunch, and we can fry eggs today instead of scramble them, because we have lard."

Kenzie exclaimed, "Yippee! I like milk. Can we drink some now?"

"I don't see why not, as long as we save some for gravy." John allowed the children to drink directly from the cup, two swallows each, two times, and they brought it down to the amount he needed for gravy. He started a fire out back, fried three eggs in the skillet, made gravy in the same skillet, and poured it over the eggs. The children said they liked the change.

John inquired, "You kids do all right while I rode on the horse today?"

Erroll answered, "Yeah, we watched the chickens but they didn't bother the garden."

"Did people try to scare you today?"

"Yeah."

"Who? Tell me about it."

Kenzie entered the conversation. "He's gonna say I bothered him, but I only talked."

"What did you say? He's a wicked step-brother?"

"I said that, but that's all."

"Is that right, Erroll?"

"She called me a full-blooded Paterson."

"Do you know what that means?"

"No, but she laughed and pointed when she said it."

"Do you know what that means, Kenzie?"

Kenzie grinned. "Not for sure, but Erroll hates it."

John smiled and responded to both children, "Kenzie's right, you are a full-blooded Paterson, Erroll, and you're a full-blooded Cox, Kenzie. You should both be proud, because not very many people can say either."

The children grumbled about the full-blooded tag, but John put out the fire and suggested some plans for the afternoon. "I'll ride the horse to the stable, then come back here. We can take the rifle and all go into the woods to try to find another squirrel, or maybe a rabbit this time, and we'll take our dirty clothes and wash them in the stream. You children can have a bath there before we come back to the shack."

Kenzie asked, "What about the garden? Will the chickens get it while we're gone?"

"We'll check just before we go. If we see chickens anywhere around, we'll chase them away. I think it's worth the risk." John took the horse to the stable and soon returned to the shack. The entire family gathered their dirty clothes and walked east to the woods. They left the clothes on the bank of the stream and enjoyed a pleasant afternoon together in the woods. They saw several squirrels, but held out for a rabbit, and eventually saw one. John shot it and they turned back toward the shack.

They crossed the stream at a shallow spot, dipped their clothes in a deeper pool, and considered them washed. They hung the clothes on tree limbs to dry, and John said he'd come back for them later. Erroll went upstream to find a place for his bath, Kenzie went downstream, and when they returned, Kenzie pointed at the stream and inquired, "Are fish in there?"

John answered, "I don't know, Kenzie. Why do you ask?"

"Can we fish in it and use Erroll for bait?"

"Of course we can't use Erroll for bait. You need to be careful what you say to your brother. Tell him you're sorry."

An impish grin spread over Kenzie's face. "He's the sorry one, not me."

Erroll pushed Kenzie into the shallow water, waded in after her, pushed her again, and both fell and got their clothes wet. John admonished the children and tried to suppress a laugh as they walked back to the shack, where he built a fire and cooked rabbit for supper.

John ate rabbit sparingly to ensure some remained. "Look, we're all full, and we still have rabbit, so I can leave some for your breakfast. That way you'll have a break from eggs."

Kenzie reacted, "Wonderful, Poppa. We'll watch the chickens again tomorrow. Do you think we'll have milk tomorrow?"

"I think so. You did a great job with the chickens yesterday. But remember, if you see anybody you don't know, forget the chickens and lock yourselves in the shack."

Erroll grinned. "We know what to do."

"Great. It's not quite dark yet. If you want to go out and play awhile, maybe your clothes will dry and I'll clean up our dishes."

The children went outside and played a running game until John called them in and put them to bed. He forgot the clothes by the stream, and didn't wait long to lie down beside Erroll and go to sleep.

Chapter 7

1887

John awakened before dawn on Wednesday, so he finished his breakfast chores and headed for the stable before sunup. He arrived at the Beauty Firth Beauties herd early, and found everybody fine. The boss predicted the men would pester John for rifle shells, and he carried some with him each day, but no one asked for any as of Wednesday.

He opened a new subject with Ron, "What do you do different with the cattle in winter?"

"We're all in our first or second month 'ere. We ain't been through a winter 'ere, so Ah don't know. Do ye know Bob? Orville?"

Nobody knew, so John hit them with another question. "What are the winters like here?"

Ron could answer that question. "They ain't bad. Th' nights are longer in winter."

"Does it get really cold? Do the streams freeze solid?" Do you get a lot of snow?"

"There's snow, but th' streams don't usually freeze and it don't get real cold 'ere."

"Do you think there's enough snow in winter the cows can't graze?"

"Yeah, prob'ly."

"Do you have hay?"

"Yeah, there's some old 'ay way up in th' valley."

"Do you have equipment to make more hay?"

"Yeah, up there by th' 'ay. There's a mower there, but it ain't no good without 'orses."

"Did anybody ever talk to you about a need for hay?" John didn't get a reply, so he continued. "I'll find out what the boss wants to do about it, and whether it involves you."

The men looked at one another, and after a hesitation, Ron spoke again. "McCarty went through 'ere chust ahead o' ye. 'E rode 'round the cattle one time, and shot on west like 'e 'uz blowed out o' a cannon."

John ignored Ron's comment and asked him another question. "What will *you* do in winter?"

"We ain't thought 'bout it. McCarty'll prob'ly fire us afore winter."

John practiced defiant talk earlier by saying the boss might have to fire him, so he practiced again. "The boss will have to fire me too, if he fires you."

Ron frowned and advised, "Don't tangle with McCarty. 'E 'd as soon fire ye as look at ye."

"Thanks Ron. Maybe I should go on and try to find him. In the meantime, you might think about how you'll keep yourselves and the cattle comfortable in winter. I'll ask you tomorrow if you thought of anything."

"Yeah, that is if ye're still 'ere tomorrow."

John grinned. "I will be. You men take care. I expect to stop on the way back east to milk the tall cow again, and will probably do that every day." He walked to his horse and rode west.

John found the herdsmen with the middle herd, and asked if they had a name for the herd. They answered Middle Valley Herd. He praised the men for the name and asked about winter, but instead of an answer, heard a warning similar to the one Ron made, that he'd see McCarty somewhere ahead. He headed west as a stiff rain began. He found the third herd where he found it the day before, and saw all three herdsmen standing in the rain. The boss faced them as he sat on a horse, and as he gestured vigorously.

John did his usual thing and got off his horse, tied him to a nearby tree, and walked over to the herdsmen. He spoke to Art and initially ignored his boss. "Morning Art. How's everything going?"

Art didn't speak, but pointed behind his back in the direction of the boss. Stan stood with the group, but shivered noticeably in the rain. The boss took charge. "John, you're way too soft on these loafers. That one," he pointed at Stan, "didn't even bother to come to work until I got here. He says he stayed in the shack yesterday and you didn't fire him."

John found himself in a put up or shut up position. "You better believe I didn't fire him. You don't fire people for being sick."

"Are you telling me what I do and don't do?"

"Maybe. One thing you don't do is fire Stan."

"I fire anybody I feel like firing."

"If you fire Stan you have to fire me too, because Art tells me Stan's a good worker. And I tell *you*, you don't need more worker turnover."

The rain fell harder and made Stan shake more violently. John turned to him. "You need to go back inside until you're well. I'll deal with the boss."

Stan didn't go, but said, "Ye don't know McCarty. 'E a'ready threatened t' fire me, and if Ah take myself off th' job, Ah'm gone."

John stood only about up to the boss's knee as he sat on his horse, but drew himself up as big as he could and bluffed, "The boss isn't going to fire anybody today, Stan. The very best thing you can do for the boss, for Art, for me, or for the cattle, is to go inside, stay dry, and get well. Now go."

Stan went, and John turned to the boss. "I don't wish to be insubordinate, Sir, but you won't fire anybody today, because you're not that ignorant of human behavior and not that lacking in human feeling. Now turn that horse around and go back to your mansion."

The boss glared. "I'll deal with you later." He spurred his horse and galloped east.

John shook almost as much as Stan, but asked Art the same questions about winter and hay he asked the other two leaders, and received about the same answers, so he asked Art to try to have suggestions on Thursday. He also asked Art about a herd name, and Art answered they decided on The Hummer Bunch, after the nearby Hummer Wood. John praised Art and his crew for the name, went by the shack to try to reassure Stan, and headed back to his own shack. He worried about Erroll and Kenzie. He didn't know if the boss would stop at the shack, and if he did, if they would bar themselves in the shack—he hoped they would—or what crazy thing the boss might do. He hurried so much to check on the children he didn't stop to milk Tall, as he called her. Rain still poured down when he rode by the shack. He saw the children inside through the open door and nothing looked amiss, so he continued up the road to the east, and went into the stable.

John found the boss in the stable, but he appeared to be on his way out of it. John called after him. "Hey, boss man."

The boss turned, stared fiercely, and growled, "I'll let you get away with today's stupidity because of Ethel—I mean Edna, but don't you ever do anything like that again."

John skipped over everything the boss said and began the same topic he pursued with the herdsmen. "How do you feed the cattle in winter when the grass is covered with snow?"

"Why do you care? I'll fire you long before snow."

"Fire me whenever you want, but we must prepare for snow before it falls."

"If you think you must know, we cut hay. The riffraff carry it by hand to a stack, and dole it back out to the cattle when they need it."

"One of them told me they need horses to pull the mowers you have out there. Where will they get the horses?"

"Don't worry your fancy head. I'll see they get horses when they need 'em. You merely do your little job and leave me alone."

John took another risk. "I'll leave you alone exactly as long as you leave my people alone."

"Where'd you get the idea they're your people?" The boss turned, went out the east door of the stable, and stomped toward his mansion. John went out the west door, breathed a sigh of relief, and walked toward his shack.

He put aside the problems of his morning when he arrived at the shack, and entered with a smile on his face. "How're you two doing today?"

Kenzie pouted, "Terrible. We had fun outside and watched the garden until it started to rain. Now we're stuck in here."

Erroll added another problem. "I wanta go to the bathroom, but can't because of the rain."

John dug around in the trunk and said, "Here's my winter coat. Maybe it will keep you dry."

Kenzie wanted the coat to make her own bathroom trip when Erroll returned. John looked out the door when the children were back in the shack. "The looks of the sky make me think the rain might go on the rest of the day, so I probably can't start a fire. I think we have to skip lunch for the day, and we don't even have milk." The children frowned about the idea, but didn't fuss.

John noted another problem. "We washed our clothes yesterday and left them by the creek. Do you think they're dry?"

Upbeat Erroll suggested, "They're under leaves. They might be."

Realistic Kenzie thought otherwise. "Why would they be dry? Did you see the rain in the sky?"

John laughed and noted, "I'm already wet, so I won't need the coat to go out. I'll go get the clothes, and we can try to invent a way to dry them inside."

He brought the clothes, draped them over the table, and they didn't dry. He told the children stories most of the afternoon, but took breaks to bring wood inside to dry and to check the wet clothes.

Rain stopped near six o'clock, so he quickly took some damp wood back outside, built a fire, fried three eggs, told a few more stories, and put the children to bed. Rain didn't resume before he went to bed, but he heard it on the roof a couple times later in the night, along with a steady drip on something inside the shack.

Rain continued Thursday morning and John's clothes remained wet. He didn't change them, but waited to leave the shack, because he couldn't start a fire. He used the time to bring more wood inside to dry and to plot a procedure to fix the roof.

Rain slowed for a while, but clouds delayed daylight that morning, and the children slept until almost eight o'clock. John greeted them when they awakened, and said he'd try to build a fire. He started a tiny fire on the shovel inside the shack, carried it barely outside the door, added wood, and fried six eggs—three for breakfast, two for the children to have for lunch, and one more for his own lunch. He told the children he already opened the chicken house door, but he thought the chickens would stay inside until the rain stopped. He suggested the children stay inside too, but since his clothes remained wet from the previous day, he went out in the rain, walked to the stable, and rode west to check on the herds.

He found Ron alone near the cattle when he came to the Beauty Firth Beauties. He greeted Ron and asked about Orville and Bob. Ron explained, "Because Ah'm a leader now, Ah telt 'em t' stay inside 'till it stops rainin'. Ah telt 'em the cattle ain't goin' nowhere anyways, and Ah can watch'em."

"Great thinking Ron. Maybe you can send Bob or Orville out the next time it rains, while you stay inside."

"Yeah, Ah might do that."

"Do you have any thoughts about hay?"

"None except we'll chust ask ye for 'orses when we think it's time t' cut grass, then let it dry, kick it up in bunches with our feet, and carry it t' small stacks we'll make."

"Great thinking again. I'll see if the boss'll provide you with a pitch-fork when the time comes, to speed up the carry step. Let me know when you think it's close to time."

"All right."

"What are the chances you'll stay after you get hay experience this year?"

"Ah only been 'ere a couple o' months. Ah'm supposin' McCarty'll fire me any time. Whether Ah go or stay is up t' 'im."

"So you intend to stay a second year if the boss doesn't fire you?"

"Yep."

"Do you know how long Bob and Orville plan to stay?"

"Nope."

"Will you try to find out? If you can persuade them to remain, it will be a feather in your hat, and your crew's experience will have value."

"Whateffer you say."

John went back to his horse and rode west to the Middle Valley Herd. He had a different conversation with Ike at the Middle Valley Herd, from the one with Ron. Ike and his crew stood together near the herd, but when John asked if everybody would continue, Ike pulled him away from the group, lowered his voice, and confided, "I hope to stay, and I hope Thomas will, but to tell you the truth, I hope Jimmy won't. He's hard to wake up in the morning, and he's a skimier, a parasite. He doesn't like work."

"You know him better'n I do, Ike. If you want him gone, fire him, but first tell him your complaints, tell him what more he needs to do to satisfy you, and give him time to do it. He might surprise you."

"I don't think he will. We'll need him to carry his share of the load when we get to the hay."

"You're right, you will. I'll leave it in your hands, but do give Jimmy some time."

"All right, I will. We're all miserable enough already, but I'll talk to him this afternoon if the rain stops."

"Good plan. I'm late today because of the rain, so I need to go." John walked to his horse and continued his ride west. He saw Art and Thomas with the Hummer Bunch, but not Stan. He asked Art, "Is Stan all right today?"

"He's a lot better, but I told him to stay in and stay dry another day. Two of us can stand here and watch the cattle as well as three of us."

John asked Art the same questions about staying he asked Ron, and heard similar answers. He dropped in on Stan to reinforce Art's instruction to stay dry, went back east, milked Tall, and went directly to the stable. He didn't make it to the stable until well after noon, walked back toward the shack, came around the end of Big Wood, and saw Erroll run from the stream to the shack. Erroll dripped water when John arrived at the shack, so he grilled him a bit. "How come you're wet, Erroll?"

"The rain did it."

"Why isn't Kenzie wet?"

"She stayed inside."

"Why'd you go down by the stream?"

"I didn't."

"I saw you there, Erroll. I know you were there."

"I chased a chicken down there."

"The chickens are all in their house. They don't come out in the rain."

"I didn't go to the stream."

"I saw you, Erroll. I don't like to leave you here alone every day, but I have to do it, and have to trust you to obey the rules. Did you fall in the water?"

"Maybe a little."

"Can I trust you to follow all the rules after today?"

"I already follow them."

"I'll never forgive myself, Erroll, if you drown in the stream while I'm gone, or if somebody wants to hurt you and catches you away from the shack. My rules aren't to make things tough for you, but to keep you alive and well. Do you understand that?"

"Yes, Poppa."

"I have to trust you, because I have to go to the herds every day. I need to trust you to follow the rules and to tell me the truth. I'll ask again, can I trust you?"

"Yes, Poppa."

Chapter 8

1887

John found dry clothes for Erroll. The rain continued past two o'clock, and he appreciated the lunch he already cooked. Rain stopped, and he suggested another hunting trip in the woods. The children left the shack dry, but came to the stream cold and soaked from the wet grass, so he allowed them to skip their bath. They walked around in the woods for a while, John shot a squirrel, and they went back to the shack; the children remained outside to play while John built a fire and cooked the squirrel. Dusk fell before he dressed the children in dry clothes and the evening meal ended; John told a couple stories and put them down for the night.

He awakened early again on Friday, saw stars all over the sky, and heard no rain on the roof. He put leftover squirrel in two pots for the children's breakfast, skipped his, cleaned up in the stream, and planted tomato seeds in eggshells before he could see. He walked to the stable when sufficient light appeared in the east, and checked out a horse for his herd visits. He rode across the Beauty Firth Beauties site before sunup, and saw the crew awake and outside their shack, but not with the cattle yet. John didn't get off his horse this time, but merely rode by and waved.

He arrived at the Middle Valley Herd earlier than usual. All three of the men stood together near the cattle, and John jumped down from his horse to talk with Ike. Ike again pulled him away from the group. "I spoke to Jimmy yesterday, and he said he'll stay today, as his last day."

"Maybe that's for the best. Can you suggest a replacement for him?"

"Hiring's your job, isn't it?"

"Officially, but if you know somebody you think'll be good, I'll go after that person."

"There's a guy named Jon McCandless in Inverness, and I know where he lives."

"Does he already have a job?"

"Not as far as I know. He'll be a good worker if we can get him."

"Tell me where to go, and I'll look for him in Inverness this afternoon."

Ike told John an address. He walked back to his horse, rode to the next herd, and found everybody at full strength, including Stan.

Stan thanked him for saving his job but John tried to be modest. "Stan, I did what I'm supposed to do. Art says you pull your weight here. I realize the boss can be a bit hasty, so I slowed him down until he thought about it, that's all."

Stan argued, "Ye done a lot more'n slow'im down, ye faced'im down. 'E might fire me yet, but Ah'll be forever grateful to ye. Ah ain't book-learnt, and this's as good a job as Ah can get. Ah need it."

"Thank you Stan." John turned toward Art, then back to Stan. "I plan to home-school my children in the fall. If you want book learning, maybe you can switch with somebody in the Beauty Firth Beauties herd, and join us."

"Ah ain't leavin' Art. 'E stood up for me too."

"If you change your mind, let me know."

"Ah ain't gonna change ma mind 'bout stayin' with Art."

"That's up to you."

John remounted his horse and headed back east. He kept moving except for a brief stop to milk Tall, and returned to his shack before noon. The children played outside. He tied the horse behind the shack again. The sun beat down all morning, the wood dried, and even the clothes inside on the table dried. He started a fire, and fried the only two eggs they had at that moment. Kenzie continued to complain about the egg diet. “I hate eggs. When can we have something else?”

Erroll reinforced Kenzie’s gripe. “I hate’em too.”

“Eggs are almost all we have, so we have to eat a lot of them. But we do have milk, and we can also have gravy today. Our little chicks will grow, and we can have fried chicken someday. Can you see anything in the garden?”

Kenzie shook her head, “No, nothing’s there, and I don’t think there ever will be.”

“Yes there will, but we must wait for it. I have to go into Inverness first thing after lunch, but will be back early, and this afternoon we can go look for another rabbit, wash clothes, and take a bath again.”

Erroll still didn’t claim to like eggs, but he endorsed the other parts of the plan. “That sounds like fun, don’t you think, Kenzie?”

“Yes, I guess so.”

Everybody disliked eggs, but they had nothing else to eat. So the children ate gravy on an egg, and John ate gravy. They washed their clothes when they first crossed the stream after lunch, so they could hang them on tree limbs earlier, and give them more time to dry than before. The children also wanted to take their baths the first time across the stream, and John allowed them to do it. They had a long lazy afternoon in the woods, and passed up a rabbit early, because they didn’t yet want to go back. They saw another later, and John shot it. They enjoyed rabbit for their evening meal, and as always, John set enough aside for the children’s breakfast the next morning. He went back to the stream for the almost-dry clothes, which he spread over the table again, and carried in more wood. He even had time to climb on the roof outside and slip a piece of tree bark into place under the roof leak.

The boss told John to visit the herds every day, but he planned to make it quick on Saturdays and Sundays, and needed to explain to his three groups of herdsmen. He called the children in before dark and told them he'd leave before they woke up the next morning, but rabbit would be on the table. He put them to bed and soon followed.

He left early again Saturday morning. He told Ron with the first herd he would sometimes merely ride through on Saturdays and Sundays, but that if Ron wanted to talk to him, he'd stop. He told Ike at the Middle Valley Herd the same thing, and he also told him he hired Jon. He said Jon planned to meet him at the stable on Sunday, and would ride double with him to the Middle Valley Herd. John continued to The Hummer Bunch after he left the Middle Valley Herd, saw Art, and repeated the message he gave Ron. He turned back east, stopped as always to fill his quart cup, and went to the stable. He returned to the shack early, and offered the children milk as a late-morning snack.

Kenzie helped drink the milk, but then ran and pointed. "Look in the garden. We have—uh—something growing." John went with Kenzie and saw peas and beans; still no potatoes. The family spent another long afternoon together, and the children acted bored with all the time they had with John. Even less happened on Sunday. Nothing unusual occurred except Jon rode to the Middle Valley Herd. John pointed out to the children, "We had problems with Uncle Eric, but in spite of him, our first week here hasn't been bad. You got along all right without me in the mornings, and we have more afternoon time together than we had in Rochester. It would be handy if cooking could be easier, but aside from that, I see only clear sailing ahead."

Kenzie argued, "We can't see anything ahead. If what's ahead means we eat more eggs, I don't want to see it."

Erroll had a rosier view. "Poppa says we have clear sailing ahead. He knows, so we do."

John grinned and responded, "Erroll, I'm glad you think I know, but Kenzie's right. None of us can know what will happen tomorrow. The best we can say is we can't see anything bad about to happen, and we can't."

Chapter 9

1887

John awakened early on his second Monday in Scotland, left scrambled eggs for the children, and went to the stable with several questions to ask Sampson, his boss's middle-aged 'stable boy.' He began as soon as he entered the stable. "Does the boss pay his herdsmen in person, or will he leave the money with me to pay them?"

Sampson's response didn't answer the question. "I never talk about Mr. McCarty's business."

John tried again. "What about horses for the herdsmen to use to cut hay. Do they get those through you?"

"I never talk about Mr. McCarty's business."

"What is it about Eric that shuts your mouth?"

"I never talk about Mr. McCarty's business."

John took a parting shot. "Have you ever met Eric McCarty?"

Sampson didn't show frustration or humor, but merely repeated, "I never talk about Mr. McCarty's business." John gave up on the questions, and saddled the horse Sampson brought. He rode away to see the herds.

He dismounted when he saw Ron and his group, and walked to the group. "Hey guys. Everything all right here today?"

Ron answered, "Right's rain."

John turned to one of his questions for the day. How often do you get paid?"

"Ah don't know. Since 'erb quit, we ain't got paid."

"Who's Herb?"

"'E's the man ye replaced."

"So Herb came around with your pay?"

"Sometimes."

"Do you know how he got the money from Eric?"

"Nope."

"How often did you get paid?"

"No set schedule. Chust wheneffer 'erb showed up with money."

"Did he pay you closer to weekly, or closer to monthly?"

"Well, Ah ain't been 'ere more'n two months. Ah been paid twice, so Ah guess it could be either."

"You should be paid on a regular and predictable schedule. Maybe I need to talk to the boss about it. I'll let you know what I find out."

"Whateffer."

"I have another question for you. What do you eat?"

"Ye mean ever' day?"

"Yes, I guess so."

"We eat eggs and milk 'most ever' day. We shoot a squirrel or rabbit 'most ever' day. We eat all right, but we ain't 'ad a tattie or a piece o' pie since we come out 'ere."

"How did you use the money when you were paid? I mean, where did you spend it?"

"We generally done different things. Ah sent mine to my mom in Inversnekle."

"Inversneckle?"

"Inverness. I sent it with 'erb."

"Can you buy food or clothing with it?"

"We might, 'cept we can't leave th' cattle."

"Do you have winter clothing out here?"

"No, but we won't need it. McCarty'll fire us afore winter."

"Just in case he doesn't, do you know how you'll keep warm?"

"Nope."

"I'll try to talk to the boss sometime this week, and will get back to you about the money."

"Aye, right. Don't waste no time worryin' 'bout it. Ah ain't."

John changed the subject. "One other thing—Mr. McCarty said you need rifle shells from time to time. How are you on those?"

"We got a coffee can in th' shack with thirty or forty. We won't need none for at least a month."

"Thanks Ron."

"Ah ain't sure for what, but ye're welcome."

John walked back to his horse and rode further west. He didn't talk to Ike or Art about pay, because he first needed to talk to his boss about it. He eventually turned around, went back east, and left milk with Erroll and Kenzie when he went by his shack. He told them he'd go on to the stable before lunch, and would even talk with Uncle Eric if he could find him, so he might be late. The children looked at each other and Erroll shook his head no, but didn't say anything, so John turned and rode to the stable.

He asked Sampson if he knew how to find the boss when he arrived at the stable, and heard the customary answer. "I never talk about Mr. McCarty's business."

"All right, if you won't talk can you give him a message for me?"

"Yeah. Write it down and I'll give it to him."

"Do you have anything to write on?"

"Maybe. Let me look." Sampson went to the back of the stable and returned with a writing tablet and a pencil.

John took the writing materials, said "Thanks," and wrote a message: 'Mr. McCarty—can we schedule regular weekly meetings? I have some questions this week, and likely will have more later.' He signed the note 'John Paterson,' and gave it to Sampson, with a question. "Can you estimate how long it might be before you can give this to Mr. McCarty?"

Sampson gave his standard reply about Mr. McCarty's business; John replied, "You're an open book of information, Sampson. I suppose I should thank you, but I can't think why," and walked back to the shack.

He greeted the children with, "Hi kids. Did everything go all right here this morning?"

Before they could answer, loud and nearby thunder cracked. Everybody laughed, and then Kenzie reported, "Uncle Eric came by here a little while before you did."

"Did you talk to him?" A sudden rain splattered them, and they went inside the shack.

Kenzie continued the conversation, but Erroll went behind Kenzie's privacy curtain, and remained there until it ended. "No, we didn't talk to him. We came in and barred the door like you told us. He saw us come in, and he knew we were in here, but we didn't talk."

"Did he talk?"

"Sort of."

"Sort of?"

"Yes, he called us names."

"What names?"

"If I tell you, you'll spank me."

"Oh. All right then, I must talk to Uncle Eric about that. You did exactly the proper thing. If he comes around here again, I want you to bar yourselves in again. You did right, and don't do differently next time. Understand?"

"I understand."

"Do you still have the milk I left?"

Erroll re-entered the conversation. "Yes, it's on the table, but we're hungry."

"How about if I make a big pot of gravy and we eat that straight, with no eggs?"

Kenzie responded, "That's all right with me, Poppa. I hate eggs." She looked out the door a moment, and elaborated, "I begs to stop eggs."

John grinned, went to the door and looked up. "The sky looks like rain might go on awhile. Maybe I can't make a fire for gravy. How will it be if you and Kenzie just drink the milk?"

Erroll said, "I like milk. Don't you, Kenzie?"

"Me too. Can we do it now? I don't want to wait longer."

John skipped lunch altogether, and the children drank milk. He asked about the garden when they finished the milk. Erroll replied, "More stuff 's up, but we don't know what. The chickens tried to look at it, but we chased them away."

"Good work Erroll. We'll eat from the garden before you know it."

Kenzie shook her head. "We saw plants up, but they're really little. I don't think any of them will get big enough for us to eat."

"We must wait and see. You might be surprised at how much food we get from there." John switched topics. "Our woodpile is down to barely over half its size when we came. We need to go back to the woods to find wood for it, and sometime before winter, a lot of wood. But we can't do it in the rain."

He moved to his rainy day procedure, and told stories until the rain stopped a couple hours later. The children wanted to look for wood the instant the rain stopped, but John persuaded them to hold off an hour for the wood and grass to dry, and the boss came back while they delayed.

John saw his boss approach on a horse, greeted him, and waited to mention what Kenzie told him about the earlier visit. "Hello Mr. McCarty. I see you got the message I left with Sampson."

"Sampson didn't give me a message but I'm here to give you one."

John replied, "Good. What is it?"

"I looked for you here this morning, and these snot-noses hid from me inside the shack. That's unacceptable, and I won't stand for it."

"Yes, they told me about your visit. I told them to bar the door when they see a visitor. They did as I instructed, and they'll do it again. If that's unacceptable, you need to take it up with me."

"See to it that it doesn't happen again."

"If you try to visit when I'm not here, it for sure will happen again. Perhaps the way out is for me to tell you my schedule, so you can visit when I'm here."

"Fine, what's your schedule?" The boss spoke as if to a child.

"I'm here in afternoons, usually by two, and then after that until morning. The message I left with Sampson asked for a meeting with you. Can we talk now?"

"Humph. I don't have time for meetings, but if you got something on your chest, let's hear it."

"My first question is about pay. How often do you pay the herdsmen?"

"Whenever I feel like doing it."

"They need a regular pay schedule that makes sense to them. Like every Friday, say, or the last day of every month."

"You been in the country a week, and you know more about how to deal with the riffraff than I do?"

"I supervised men for years, Sir, and yes, I do know things you don't. I know your employees won't respect you if you don't respect them, and I know part of that respect includes paying them on a regular schedule."

"So when do you want to pay them?"

"How about every Friday?"

"Do you have money to pay them?"

"They're your employees, Sir. You should pay them."

"Exactly. They're my employees, and it's none of your business."

"If you want me to represent you, it's my business too."

"If it wasn't for Esther, or Ethel, or Edna, or whoever, I'd fire you on the spot. But I'll leave riffraff money with Sampson on Fridays."

"Thank you, Mr. McCarty. That's a wise choice."

"I already said I'll leave the money on Fridays. Stop the blether about it."

Chapter 10

1887

"Yes Sir." John wanted to ask more questions, but held them for a better time. The boss, still on a horse, rode back toward the stable.

The children went out to play while John and his boss talked. John allowed them to play until the grass dried, and then proposed again they go to the woods to pick up firewood. Kenzie reacted, "Great. We like to walk in the woods, don't we, Erroll." She phrased her last sentence as a question, but made it sound more like a statement.

Erroll agreed and followed with a true question. "Yeah. Can we go now?"

"Sure, come on." They left the shack and walked toward the woods. They crossed the stream at their customary shallow place, and John suggested they carry wood back across the stream, carry it up a little rise, and leave it there. John and the children worked until Kenzie complained, and they amassed a good-sized pile of wood.

John instructed, "You kids go on back to the shack and play. I'll carry this wood up to it." He carried it all before he stopped, put about half the wood inside, and rebuilt the outside pile to almost its original size. He fried six eggs, for both supper and the next morning's breakfast, and called the children in. They were so hungry they ate eggs without their usual complaint, and went back outside to play.

John continued to try to improve working conditions for the herdsmen. He told Ron, Ike, and Art what the boss promised about their pay. His conversation with Art prompted a couple more thoughts. "Mr. McCarty says he'll leave your pay with Sampson each Friday. Ron over at the Beauty Firth Beauties Herd and Ike at the Middle Valley Herd, say it doesn't matter much, because they can't get away to pick up their money, so they agreed I should bring it to them and to their crews each Friday. You want me to do the same for you and your crew?"

Art shrugged. "That's all right with me, and I suppose with Stan and Thomas too. But what does it matter if we have money here? What can we use it for?"

John tried to answer Art's question by asking another. "How often do you have a day off you can use to go into Inverness to buy things?"

"I never heard about a day off. Either we don't get 'em, or none of us've been here long enough to get one. And if we get one, it'll take all day to walk to Inverness and back."

"Then I don't suppose you get a vacation either?"

"Not as far as I know."

"Those are a couple more things I need to talk to the boss about. In the meantime, if you need food or anything else I can buy for you in Inverness, do you want to give me money and have me buy it and bring it to you?"

Art's face looked positive for the first time during the conversation. "I know there's things we want if we have a way to get them. Can I talk to Thomas and Stan about it? We still have money Herb brought, and if we get more, we can tell you some things when it happens."

"That'll be great, Art. I'll talk to you about that, and there's one other thing. Do you three ever participate in a special activity, maybe a ball game, music event, or picnic while on the job?"

"I ain't seen it. But I heard tales some people from a kirk come by here with a wagon and put on a feed for us every summer. We been on the edge of hungry since we come out here. A big feed to fill us up'll feel really good."

"Do you know where the wagon comes from?"

"I ain't seen no wagon, but I suppose it comes from Ingersneck-le."

"I'll look into it if I get a chance."

Thomas and Stan listened to the entire conversation between John and Art, but neither spoke until the end, when Thomas confirmed, "Yeah, I heard about the wagon too. We'll turn flips if it brings real food out here." John repeated he'd look into it, got on his horse, and went back east toward his shack. A light rain began as he rode, but ended before he came to the Beauty Firth Beauties Herd. He stopped to milk Tall, and while there, he asked Ron if his mom knew about the kirk wagon Art heard tales about.

"Aye. Ma mom goes t' that kirk, called Tiny Kirk. They send a wagon ever' summer. They go t' McCarty's 'erds first, on past Beauty Firth, then south 'most t' Drumnadrochit afore they turn back north-east t' Inversneckle. They take most o' th' summer t' do it. Ma mom don't go, but she always donates food t' th' wagon."

"Can you tell me how to find your mom? I'd like to talk to her about it if you think it'll be all right."

Ron provided his mom's address and her name, Kalindra Everett. So after John cooked lunch for the children, he walked to Inverness, and learned the wagon would leave about the middle of May. He noted the current date of May three, and figured the wagon would leave within two weeks. He thanked Mrs. Everett, tried to explain the need to her, and turned toward his shack.

The rain didn't resume that day, but a bigger problem happened. John skirted Big Wood after he left Inverness, and heard the boss in the direction of his shack yelling obscene names. He ran toward the shack and found the boss outside the door, red-faced and shaking with anger.

The boss couldn't talk in a normal tone, he could only yell because of his anger. "You said you're always at your shack by two o'clock, but it's 2:30 now. If those kids of yours lock me out of the shack that I own again, I'll burn it down with them in it." The boss emphasized the words 'I own,' and pointed to himself as he said them.

John's alarm first built faster than his anger. Alarm remained, but anger flared. "You're doomed if you harm one hair on my children's head. You better not ever do it. Not ever. Do I need to go to the law to protect my children?"

The boss continued to shake. "I own that shack. Those kids have no right to keep me out."

"Boss, as long as we live there we have every right to keep you out. I instructed my children to keep out anyone they have reason to fear, and I don't intend to change that instruction. If you return when I'm not here, they'll do it again. They'll do it a hundred times if you make them do it, because I won't change my instruction."

"It's my shack. I own it."

John increased his voice volume to a yell. "When you talk to my children treat them with respect. If you must cuss somebody, cuss me. But I won't have you cussing my children. Do you understand that?"

"I'll cuss anybody I want to."

"Not my children you won't. Have you got that?"

"It's my shack. I own—"

John didn't let his boss shift the subject. "Have you *got* that?"

"Will you stop talking about those knot heads?" The boss continued to yell and to shake with crazed anger.

"They're children. Have you got what I said?"

The boss seemed to shrink a little. "I got it. And I got the message you left with Sampson. Do you want to talk to me or not?"

John said with a slightly calmer tone, although he remained mad, "We do need to talk, but must do it at your stable. I don't want you around my children again, ever."

"I don't understand what's the big deal about those knot heads."

"They're children. And I don't expect you to understand much of anything. Do you want to talk, or not?"

"I'll talk." They walked away from the shack, toward the stable.

John didn't wait until they reached the stable. "Your herdsmen need a regular day off, at least during the summer when they're not busy. And a paid week of vacation too."

"John, you're way too soft on no-goods like those. You give'em a day off, they'll want two. There's no end to what they might want, except to not work and to not earn their pay."

"Mr. McCarty, I don't know if their pay is a sacrifice for you or not, but I do know it costs you in reduced performance when you have to replace somebody. Your men'll work for you, but their willingness will fade unless you show them it pays off."

"My liveryman doesn't get a day off. My stable boy doesn't. Why should my herdsmen?"

" Maybe you have it backwards. Maybe you should ask, if it's good for the herdsmen, why isn't it good for all your employees?"

"Are you asking for a day off?"

"I'm not asking, but it would be nice. What I'm asking is a day off every week for your herdsmen. Do you know each group of your herdsmen has chosen a crew leader and a name for their herd?"

"So why do I care about that?"

"It's up to you whether you care, but I'll tell you the names if you want to know."

"If it makes you happy."

John told his boss the three herd names, the three crew leader names and the names of all his other herdsmen. He also told him Jimmy quit and Jon replaced him.

"You mean only one man quit in the past week? Usually half of'em quit every week."

"That's because I've talked about you as a halfway decent man. You need to prove me right."

"And be a mush-head like you?"

"And be whatever you want to call it. What about the days off?"

"I'll think about it."

"For how long?"

"Till I decide, that's how long."

"How will you let me know what you decide?"

"I'll come by the shack after two o'clock a few days after I decide."

"That won't work. I told you never to go to the shack again, remember?"

"I'll go to the shack whenever I want to. I own it."

"You won't go to it as long as I live there. I'll come out and beat you to a pulp if I'm there, and the children will lock you out if I'm not there. We must meet in the stable."

"Those snot-noses better not lock me out."

"The stable, Eric."

"I'm Mr. McCarty to you. All right, the stable."

"If you tell Sampson when you decide, and when you want to meet, I'll be there."

"See that you are."

John turned to go to his shack and his boss continued east toward the mansion.

Kenzie and Erroll acted proud of their door-bar behavior when John returned, and he praised them for it. "Great work kids. You did exactly the right thing. I talked to Uncle Eric about it today, and I don't think he'll do it again. But we're going to make a little door in the back wall of the shack, just in case. If he ever comes back, bar the door, go out the new door, and run up the hill while you stay behind the shack where he can't see you. When you get to the trees, turn and run into the main woods. If he chases you, hide from him there. Nobody's ever supposed to know about the door, just us."

John suggested the children bar the door again. Then he took them behind Kenzie's privacy curtain, moved her bed away from the wall, and used his pocketknife to cut little chunks from a board in the south wall of the shack until he cut through it. He instructed Kenzie and Erroll to pick up the wood chunks and put them in a pile on the table. After he cut through the board, John unbarred the door, went outside, and pushed inward on the cut board until it broke off at the floor.

He put the board back in place, pushed the bed against it to hold it, and showed the children how to move the bed, pull the board toward them, and crawl out of the shack. He had each of them practice it a couple times. He continued to worry about his boss, but knew Erroll and Kenzie could escape if they had to do it. He closed the new door and put everything back in order, then told the children scatter the wood chips outside.

The children helped him carry more firewood from across the stream as the week went along, and they continued to complain about eggs.

When John went to the stable for his horse on Friday, Sampson showed him ten piles of money, one for each of the herdsmen, and one for him. He took the money and disbursed proper amounts to the herdsmen as he came to them. John asked each crew leader to confirm his men wanted him to shop for them in Inverness. Even before they all did, he suggested everyone keep his money until later; he would shop for Art's group Monday, for Ike's group Tuesday, and for Ron's Wednesday. He didn't mention days off because he didn't have an answer from his boss yet. When he rode by the shack on the way to return the horse, he stopped to ask the children to put the milk on the table, to tell them he had two weeks pay, and would walk into Inverness before he returned. The boss waited at the stable when John arrived there. He told John he decided to give each herdsman a day off each week, but would not grant one to him, and would not allow him to check horses out of the stable for herdsmen to ride. John only wanted days off for the herdsmen, so the prohibitions didn't bother him. He thanked the boss and walked on to Inverness, where he bought food to add to the children's milk and egg diet.

He returned to the shack late because of his trip to Inverness, but had food he expected the children to like. "Hey kids, look what I bought in Inverness."

Erroll pointed and asked, "What's that?"

"That's a ham. We have enough to last days and days." John intended to save most of it for the children. "And here are potatoes. We won't plant these. We'll eat them."

Kenzie responded, "Yipee! Can we eat now, Poppa?"

John combined the noon and evening meals, because he wanted a big one, and suspected the children did too. "I need to build a fire to cook the potatoes and part of the ham, but we can eat as soon as I do that."

They finished eating early, and the children went outside afterward with plenty of time to play. John washed the dishes, took the children down to the stream for a bath, and they played more until their bedtime. He saved part of his wage for the rug he saw, but still didn't have enough to buy it. He told the children about it, and told them he hoped he could buy it before winter. But he also informed them he needed to save enough to buy shoes for all three of them before winter.

John and his boss accommodated one another better after their argument on Friday. The boss didn't come closer to the shack than the road past it, and John didn't pester the boss about plans for vacation and hay.

The Tiny Kirk wagon stopped at John's shack a little before noon on a day in May; the children first barred the door, but yielded to promises of food and soon opened it. John arrived during the middle of the children's meal and also received food. They ate as much as they could hold, and the children begged the Tiny Kirk people to park the wagon by their shack for the summer. John tried to explain the larger need to them, but suspected they focused their desire only on their own need.

John walked into Inverness on Fridays to shop for his family, and on Mondays through Wednesdays for the herdsmen. He kept items he bought for the herdsmen in the shack until the next day.

Ike brought up an old topic in early June. "Grass is ready to cut whenever you can get horses to pull the mower."

"I'll leave a message for the boss. I suppose he's as interested as you are, although he may not know as much about hay as you. I don't know how long it will take him to tell me anything."

"The cattle are his. If he doesn't care about them, why should we?"

"I understand, Ike. Again, I think he might listen to a message from you. I'll try."

"All right."

John left a message with Sampson that day when he took the horse back to the stable, and only a couple days later, Sampson said Mr. McCarty wanted him to take two extra horses from the stable for the herdsmen to watch over for three weeks—no more, no less—to pull the mowers. So John led two harnessed horses with him to the Middle Valley Herd, and relayed his boss's instructions to Ike.

Ike complained about the time limit. "We might cut our hay in three weeks, but because it rains so often, we might have to wait for it to stop."

John knew nothing about hay, but knew his boss. "Plan to keep the horses a week, and then I'll take them on to The Hummer Bunch for a week. Mow hay in the rain if you must, but do it in one week."

Ike shrugged and turned away. "We'll get pathetic quality, but whatever you say."

"Good. I'll tell Art to expect the horses a week from now, and Ron two weeks from now."

John told Ike he didn't want to ask the boss for a pitchfork, but he knew the hay work would go better if the herdsmen had one. So when he returned to the stable he asked Sampson, "You have any spare pitchforks the herdsmen can use to move hay?"

"Yeah, I got one. The herdsmen use it every year. I let them borrow it, and don't need it much in the summer anyway, but if the fork's gone when I need it, I substitute the manure fork I use to muck out the stable. I'll get the fork for you."

The herdsmen cut all the hay they thought they needed for winter. Rain fell on most of it before it was dry enough to stack, but the crews finished with the horses in three weeks, and John took them back to the stable at the end of the specified time. The herdsmen also developed a savings program—consisting of three places in each shack to stash money—to accumulate enough to buy winter clothes in the fall.

John's garden produced during the summer, peas first, then green beans and cucumbers, followed by potatoes, and later, navy beans. Summer food did nothing but improve, but John feared winter. He saved most of the potatoes and most of the navy beans, and suggested to each group of herdsmen that come spring, they also plant a garden.

John talked with Ron about another topic during the middle part of the summer. "Ron, I'm concerned about winter. Do you have any idea how to heat your shack?"

"Nope."

"I can't feel right about you growing icicles on your beard when you try to sleep, or about my children shivering in the cold while I'm gone from our shack."

"Ye 'ave children? Ye 'ave a wife?"

"Yes, I have children. Didn't I tell you?"

"Maybe. That means ye 'ave a wife, right?"

"I had a wife back in the US named Edna, Eric's sister. But she's dead now."

"McCarty's sister? She must 'ave been awful. Did ye shoot'er?"

"No! She and Eric are like day and night. Sometimes I wonder how they can be related."

"She must 'ave been more like 'er paw. Ah 'eard 'e 'uz a great guy. Folks 'round 'ere wonder 'ow 'e and 'is son can be related. Anyway, there's no stove and not even a chimney in th' shack, so Ah think all we can do is wear a lot o' clothes."

"Wow. Can you afford to buy that stuff?"

"Nope."

John responded, "Maybe it'll work to carry up rocks to heat in a fire outside, then somehow move them inside."

"Don't sound practical t' me."

John stared into space a moment. "I don't have any ideas. Maybe I'll ask Sampson if he knows how people did it last year."

"Sampson gets t' sleep in th' stable with th' 'orses. What can 'e know 'bout it?"

"Maybe nothing, but I'll ask him. I'll think about it and if you and Bob and Orville think about it too, maybe we'll come up with something."

Chapter 11

1887

John had conversations with Ike McCord and with Art Alston about keeping warm in winter, similar to the discussion he had with Ron Everett at the first herd. Art claimed Stan's dad was a mason, however, so Stan might know how to make a fireplace. John didn't follow up immediately on the information about Stan, but talked with Sampson first. He saw Sampson when he returned his horse, and brought up the shack heat subject. "Do you know how the herdsmen keep warm in their shacks in the winter?"

"They don't."

"How do they stay alive?"

"They quit, sometimes a whole crew at a time. It will be up to you to hire replacements, until you quit too."

"Does the boss know about this?"

"I never talk about Mr. McCarty's business."

John slammed his hand on a stable pen board. "Do you refuse to talk for a reason?"

"If you don't know, I can't explain it."

"All right, so there's no plan for herdsmen to stay warm in winter?"

"I never talk about Mr. McCarty's business."

John didn't reply. He turned, left the stable, and because it was Friday, walked into Inverness. He bought food first, and enough money remained he could buy the rug he wanted.

He showed the children the food he bought when he came home, along with the rug. Erroll exclaimed about the rug. "That's gonna feel good, Poppa! The wood floor is kind o' hard."

Kenzie hopped up and down and asked about the food. "Can we eat bread and ham and beans right now? Maybe we still have to eat eggs, but I'm glad we have something to mix with them."

"Not this very minute." John paused and changed the subject. "Do the chickens still want in the garden?"

Erroll stepped in front of Kenzie. "I chased them away twice today, and Kenzie did once."

Kenzie pushed Erroll aside. "I chased them away twice too, and helped Erroll another time."

John smiled. "The important thing is you kept them out. Did anything else happen here today?" Both children looked bored, but neither answered. "Do you think we have enough wood for now?"

Erroll and Kenzie answered at the same time. "No." and "Yes."

"Do you want to go into the woods today and see if we can find some more?"

The children answered in unison again, and agreed this time. "No."

John changed the subject yet again. "You won't be six years old until January, but do you think you can begin school in September, while you're five?"

Kenzie hopped up and down again. "Yay! Where is the school?"

"Right here. You can learn at home in a home school."

"Why can't we go to a real school?" Erroll's eager look changed to a bored one.

"Your school here will be a real school." John emphasized 'will.'

Kenzie frowned and pouted, "Yes, but we won't be able to make friends and play with other kids."

John waited at least two seconds to answer. "That's right, but it won't matter. Do you know Erroll's mother went to school at her home up in the McCarty mansion? She traveled across the ocean and met people from all over the world—even me."

Kenzie continued to pout, "Yes, but I want friends now. I don't want to wait until I'm a grown up lady to have friends. Erroll sort of halfway works as a brother, but I want real friends. Girls."

"Maybe you ought to go out and check the chickens. If they're not close to the garden, then you and Erroll can play outside for a while."

"Wanta go Erroll?"

"Yep."

The children went outside, and John looked at the books in the shack; he saw the books they brought from Rochester, and no others. Not a science or math book in the bunch, so he'd need to devise something on his own. He took a first step toward school the next morning, when he went to the stable and asked Sampson, "You know the writing tablet and pencil you sometimes get for me to write messages to the boss?"

"Yes."

"Do you have enough of those you can give me some for Erroll and Kenzie to use in school?"

Sampson raised his hands and dropped them. "No way. Mr. McCarty only gives me as many of those as he thinks I need. I'd have to ask him for more, and I won't do that."

"Will it be all right if I ask him?"

"It might be your biggest and last mistake."

John grinned disbelievingly, and asked, "Do you know where I can get stuff like that?"

"You go into Inverness and spend money every week don't you? Go spend some of it on things to write with."

"That should work Sampson. I'm not crazy about the idea, but I don't have a better one."

Sampson spoke again, after a pause. "I can't help you with the tablets but Mr. McCarty gives me pencils every few months. I don't write much, so a pencil lasts years. I have a couple boxes of them in back, and you can have one if you want."

"Great. Thanks a bunch, Sampson."

John turned to go, but Sampson called him back. "I also have a box of used brown paper bags. I burn paper bags every couple of years or so, but won't this year if you want those too."

"Great Sampson. Those will be perfect. When can I pick up that stuff?"

"Right now if you want it now." Sampson gave John a box with a dozen pencils in it and another box with paper bags in it. He asked Sampson to continue to save the paper bags, and delayed his horse checkout until he went back to the shack to leave the pencils and the paper bags. He hid the materials under the table quietly, so as to not awaken the children, and went back to the stable.

John talked to Art a few minutes that day; Art told him he didn't know of any problem with the crew or the cattle. Stan stood beside them, so John merely turned to him when he finished talking with Art. "Art told me your dad's a mason, and you might know something about fireplaces. Is that right?"

"Well, Ah might know a wee bit, but only a wee bit. Why ye wanta know?"

"Art and I talked about how you three and the other crews can keep warm in winter. I know staying warm isn't a problem now, but it will turn into one before we know it."

Stan looked down and then shook his head. "We ain't talked 'bout it. We don't expect t' still be 'ere by winter anyways."

"That's terrible, Stan. Why not?"

"McCarty'll fire us afore then."

"He'd better not. But even if the worst happens, somebody'll need to keep warm. Do you think a fireplace is the best answer?"

"Ah cain't think o' no other."

"Can you make a fireplace?"

"Sort o'."

"Sort of?"

"Yeah. A real fireplace'd 'ave cut stanes or bricks, and real mortar. All Ah got 'ere's round-edge stane*s* and mud."

"Can you make that work?"

"Yeah."

"Tell me about it."

"We'll 'ave to get stanes t' block up th' middle o' th' floor, and then cut out th' wood there—"

John interrupted. "Why in the middle of the floor? Won't it be better to put it by a wall and let the chimney go up outside?"

"Not really. All th' stanes in th' flue'll be 'ot or at least warm. So if they're inside, they'll 'elp warm th' shack. And since we only got mud instead o' real mortar, we'll wanta get all 'round th' flue t' re-mud 't ever' year or so. Anything outside in th' rain 'll need re-muddin' after 'most ever' rain. The flue'll need t' stick up 'igher 'n th' peak o' th' shack. So if it comes through th' roof in th' middle, at th' top o' th' gable, th' outside part can be shorter."

"I'm dumb as a post compared to you. How can you make it?"

"Ah'll 'ave t' cut a 'ole in th' floor where Ah want th' fireplace t' be. Ah'll 'ave t' cut a floor joice under th' wood floor, but first Ah'll 'ave to block up what'll become th' joice ends. Then Ah'll 'ave to fill up th' 'ole with stanes. Ah can use little'uns for that, but bigger'uns'll be better t' make th' actual fireplace. Then Ah'll need stanes for th' flue. Ah could build a flue straight up, but it'll be solider if Ah make it as wide as th' fireplace at th' bottom, then taper it in as Ah go up. It ought 'o stick up at least a foot over th' top 'o th' roof. If Ah can get a metal pipe for that top foot, then we won't 'ave t' worry 'bout mud washin' out up there."

"What tools will you need?"

"A reg'lar carpenter saw'll be good for cuttin' th' 'ole in th' floor. If Ah's gonna do 't—finish 't—afore winter, Ah could use a wheelbarrow t' 'aul stanes from th' bluff over there." Stan pointed. "'Elp from Art and Thomas on th' 'aulin' part'll speed it up too."

John looked around the circle of men. "Does that sound like the best plan to you, Art?" Art nodded.

"To you, Thomas?" Thomas nodded too.

"Then let's do it. I need a fireplace too. Can you go over to The Middle Valley Herd on Monday, Stan, to explain how to make it? You can ride double with me on the horse to get there but will have to walk back." Stan nodded yes.

"That's great. I'll ask Ron from the Beauty Firth Beauties to send somebody from his crew on Monday too. I think I can afford to buy a handsaw for us to pass around. I'll do that Monday, and will also see what it costs to get us a wheelbarrow. I'll know the cost the next day, and will ask you if you're willing to help buy a wheelbarrow we can pass around too. In the meantime, maybe you can pile up rocks at the bottom of the bluff, or even carry them across the stream. Does that sound like the way to do it?" John looked around the circle again, and everybody nodded.

He went back to his shack, but stopped at each of the other two herds, and explained what happened at the Hummer Bunch. Nobody expected to still be employed on the McCarty estate by winter, but all agreed to start on a fireplace in their own shack.

John stopped by his shack on the way to the stable. He put the cup of milk on the table, and explained to the children he would go to Inverness, and would be a little later than they otherwise might expect. The children grumbled, but he went to Inverness anyway, bought a handsaw, and found a solid-looking wheelbarrow priced in pounds equivalent to about eighteen US dollars. He went to a grocery store on his way out of Inverness, and spent wildly on two oranges to take home to the children. He kept the oranges in his pocket when he returned to the shack, hung the handsaw on a hook on the wall, and asked, "Did anything happen here today?" The children told him about chasing the chickens away from the garden and then jumped immediately to questions about the handsaw.

John didn't answer about the handsaw, but instead went out to build a fire in front of the shack to cook lunch. He talked to the children about a fireplace while he worked on the fire and waited for it to get hot. "Are you warm enough here today?"

Erroll's eyes widened, and his hand touched his head. "Poppa, we're hot here today."

"Yes, but you might not be hot in the winter, when there's snow on the ground."

"Will we really have snow? Yipee!" Kenzie jumped up and down.

He didn't respond to Kenzie's question, but continued with Erroll. "Do you remember the big stove we had in Rochester? The one we put coal into in winter, the one that kept us warm?"

Erroll answered, "Yes, will we have one of those next winter?"

"No. That's what I want to talk to you about." He continued a few minutes about a fireplace, but went inside for the skillet and foods when the fire was hot enough, and postponed the later part of his fireplace explanation. They finished eating, and John gave an orange to each child. They squealed and gobbled them down; they hadn't seen an orange since they left Rochester.

John came back to the fireplace discussion after he cleaned up the dishes. "We won't have a furnace so we'll need something else when winter comes. I talked with the herdsmen today and they suggested a fireplace. Would you like to help build a fireplace?"

Kenzie jumped up and down again, and yelled, "Yay!" She waited a moment, and added, "Hurray!"

Erroll was only slightly more restrained. He didn't jump, but repeated Kenzie's exclamation, "Yay! Can we start now? What's a fireplace?"

John tried to apply brakes. "We can't start to build, but we can start to plan now. A fireplace is a bunch of rocks we can pile up inside our shack to contain a fire to keep us warm in winter, and we can cook in it too. Where do you think we should put it?"

Kenzie pointed and urged, "Close to my bed."

Erroll shook his head and proposed, "Outside, so we won't have smoke in here."

Kenzie asked an additional question. "Where will we get the coal?"

John tried to address all the thoughts, starting with Kenzie's question. "We'll use wood instead of coal, so we need more wood up here before winter. But we don't want the fireplace outside. We'll use a chimney like we had in Rochester, to make the smoke go outside, up above the roof. And by your bed might work Kenzie, but it will work better if we put it in the middle of the shack, where the table is now."

"Will we still have a table?"

"Oh yes. We'll still have this one, but we can move it. Do you have any ideas where we can put it?"

Kenzie brightened a bit. "Maybe we can put the table by my bed."

John turned, "Erroll?"

"There won't be room for it in the shack. Maybe we can put it outside."

"The fireplace won't be huge. What do you think about putting the table beside the fireplace, either on this side," John pointed east, "or that side?" He pointed west.

Kenzie pointed to the east. "This side, by my bed."

Erroll pointed west. "That side, by the chickens."

"Maybe we can practice and try it by Kenzie's bed today, by the chickens tomorrow, and switch back and forth until we settle on a best side."

Erroll asked, "Can we start to make the fireplace right now?"

John didn't directly answer, but continued with a question of his own. "Do you know what a fireplace looks like, or how big it is?"

"No." Kenzie went behind her privacy curtain, but John talked through it.

"I know what they look like, but I don't know how big ours will be. One of the herdsmen does know, and I'll ask him tomorrow. Step one will be to cut a hole in the floor with this saw," John pointed even though Kenzie couldn't see, "but we want to cut it the right size the first time. We don't know the right size today, so we must wait. We'll make the fireplace with rocks, so one thing we can do today is go down to the stream and throw some rocks out of it, up this way. Do you want to help with that?"

The children claimed they did want to help, and went down to the stream, but they quickly tired of the work and went back up to the shack to guard the garden and to play. John worked with the rocks a couple more hours before he joined them at the shack.

Chapter 12

1887

John didn't take the saw with him to the herds the next day, because it was Sunday. He arrived at the Hummer Bunch early, talked briefly to Art, and then asked Stan about the size of hole needed. "We won't need a big fireplace t' 'eat a shack. But a big base'll be more stable. Do ye think it'll work t' make th' fireplace two feet by two feet and th' base three feet by three feet?"

"I have no idea, Stan. If that's what you think, it sounds all right to me."

"Ah think that'll work."

"Good. I went to Inverness yesterday to buy a saw and look at wheelbarrows, even though I said I'd wait until tomorrow. Stan, you'll be at the Middle Valley Herd on Monday, right?" Stan nodded yes. "Somebody from the Beauty Firth Beauties'll be there too. If you decide there who gets the saw first, I'll take it wherever you choose, on Tuesday."

John returned to his own shack with milk before the children awakened, but he found them up when he came back from the stable, so he read to them from the Bible and then prepared breakfast. He asked them to help him estimate and draw out a three-foot square on the floor, before they went out to open the chicken house door and to play. Pegs in the floor showed floor joist locations, and they drew a square that cut across only one joist.

The children wanted to see the hole and Erroll asked, "Can we cut it now Poppa?"

"Yes, can we?"

"Not on Sunday. And we can't begin first thing after I come back tomorrow, because I have to go to Inverness after I take the horse to the stable, buy a wheelbarrow, and shop for the Hummer Bunch. But as soon as I do all that, we can put rocks under the floor to hold it up, then cut the hole. I promise." John did only domestic tasks that afternoon, including fry two eggs for the children's Monday breakfast.

He slipped out early Monday to avoid waking the children, walked to the stable, received a horse, made the short ride to the Beauty Firth Beauties, continued to the other herds, and returned to his shack, where he reminded the children he planned to go into Inverness. He returned his horse, and walked to town.

Erroll and Kenzie confronted him when he came back to the shack. Kenzie jumped up and down and begged, "Can we cut the hole now?"

Erroll repeated, "Can we?"

John reminded the children they should eat first. Kenzie accused, "You said we could cut the hole when you came back from town. You promised."

Erroll backed her up. "Yes, you promised."

"Well, I did, but we have to eat first. How about if we make our lunch quick and have only milk and tomatoes? We can have those in about five minutes."

The children grumbled, but accepted the lunch arrangement and John invited, "I have to take the wheel barrow down by the stream and get two big rocks to hold up the floor before we cut a hole in it. Do you want to go?"

They did want to go, so everybody went, loaded two flat rocks into the wheelbarrow, and John pushed the wheelbarrow behind the shack. They looked for a place to crawl under the shack, but Kenzie stated an obvious problem. "It's too low. There's not room for any of us to crawl under, not even me."

John pointed to a location. "Try there, I think you can squeeze through."

Kenzie didn't approach the low spot. "No I can't, and there might be a snake or a spider under there."

John gave up, pointed to Erroll, and jerked his head toward the low place, but Erroll responded, "Not me. I don't like snakes or spiders either."

John didn't want to force a reluctant child under, so he agreed. "You might be right, and we probably can't push a rock under with a stick, either. We'll have to cut a small hole in the floor, then put the rocks through it from inside before we cut the bigger hole." They went in the shack, John cut an opening for the two rocks, and slid them under the joist. He looked at Kenzie, then at Erroll. "Do you think we should go ahead and cut the hole now?"

Erroll frowned and blinked a couple times. "I thought you already did cut the hole."

Kenzie pointed at the opening and declared, "That's a hole, Poppa, right there."

He explained to the children, "We're going to cut a joist. We cut an opening so we can put rocks under the unsupported ends of it—the ends that will remain after we cut a chunk out of it. Joists are the big boards, or beams, that hold up the floor boards."

"Oh." Erroll answered, but puzzled looks remained on both children's faces.

John cut the joist along one of the marks on the floor, and less than ten minutes later he finished the roughly three-foot by three-foot opening. He looked at Erroll and asked, "Does that look right?"

"I think it does, Poppa. It's where you marked."

"Does it look right to you Kenzie?"

"Yes, Poppa."

"What should we do next?"

Both children shrugged. Neither spoke, so John did. "We need to fill that hole with rocks for the fireplace to sit on; we can go down to the rocky bottom of the stream for them. Do you want to go?"

Erroll muttered without enthusiasm, "Yes."

Kenzie disagreed. "I don't want to go. I got tired of rocks on Saturday."

Kenzie's answer prompted Erroll to change his yes to a no. John tried to tempt the children, "We'll get to use the new wheelbarrow. You sure you don't want to go and help push?"

Erroll didn't. "Nope."

Kenzie said, "Me neither."

John shrugged and went alone to the stream, loaded the wheelbarrow with rocks, brought the rocks to the shack, and unloaded them into the hole. He did that several times, until he filled the hole. He finished a little later than his normal time to cook, and grumbled about fatigue to the children. Nevertheless, he built a fire and cooked the evening meal, then fried two eggs for the children's breakfast on Tuesday, watched them play outside for another hour, and finally suggested they all go to bed. He claimed the new thick rug felt even better than on previous nights.

John woke up early Tuesday morning. He took the handsaw off the hook, went quietly out the door, and looked at the wheelbarrow a moment. Then he carried the saw to the stable, climbed on a horse, and rode to the Beauty Firth Beauties herd with the handsaw, but without the wheelbarrow.

He came to the first crew and spoke to Bob. "Did you decide where the handsaw'll go first?"

"Yes, we think you can have it first, since you bought it."

"I already used it—did it yesterday. Did you decide where to send it next?"

"We think Stan can use it after you, and then you can bring it back to the Middle Valley Herd, and finally to us."

"That works for me. I have the saw and I'll take it all the way to the Hummer Bunch today."

He saw Sampson when he first entered the stable, they engaged in small talk, and then John asked, "Do you have a rope I can use to pull a wheelbarrow off and on for pretty much the rest of the summer?"

"Rope?"

John explained, "Yes, I want to pull a wheelbarrow behind a horse, and drop it off with each crew at various times during the summer."

Sampson's face looked like it might if a horse stood on his foot. "There's plenty of rope in the stable, but it all belongs to Mr. McCarty."

"Can you let me use it and not tell the boss?"

"Are you crazy? What if he finds out? No, I can't do it."

"I don't want to get you in trouble. Maybe I can afford to buy rope in Inverness."

"Can you cut a long slim sapling with a hook on the end and use that instead of a rope?"

"I never thought about that, but it might work. I'll see what I can find when I get back to the shack."

John thought about Sampson's idea while he walked to Inverness to buy groceries for Ike's crew, and used his own money to buy two feet of light cord.

He returned to his shack and prepared lunch, then invited the children to get away from the shack for a while. "We haven't walked in the woods lately. Do you want to do that today?"

Kenzie jumped two times, and added an extra idea. "Yay! You can take the gun and shoot a squirrel, so we can have meat for supper."

Erroll contributed, "Yeah! Let's do it!"

"Our little chickens are big enough I think we can have fried chicken tonight instead of squirrel. Do you prefer that?"

Kenzie asked, "What does fried chicken taste like?"

"You don't remember? It tastes like squirrel."

Erroll responded, "Let's do the squirrel."

Chapter 13

1887

"All right, we'll do the squirrel. I also want to find a little tree I can cut down with my pocketknife. Are you ready to go?"

Erroll asked, "Will the chickens hurt the garden while we're gone?"

"I hope they won't. We can make sure they're not close before we leave. Maybe next year we should put the garden way down by the road, where the chickens don't often go."

Kenzie asked the next question, "Yeah, can we go now?" The Patersons took their dirty clothes along, and washed them in the stream before they crossed into the woods. John shot a squirrel during their first minutes there, but the children still had excess energy, and he hadn't found the right wood to cut. He eventually found a straight sapling with a downward-sloping limb about ten feet off the ground. He cut it with his pocketknife and trimmed all the limbs off it, except he left about six inches of the downward-sloped limb. He found another, also with a downward limb, and cut it like the first, except only about three feet long. John carried the squirrel and the saplings back to the shack when the children finished playing in the woods. They took their clean clothes off the tree limbs and carried those back to the shack as well.

John built a fire in front of the shack and cooked the squirrel, along with garden produce. They ate their meal, he saved some squirrel for the children's breakfast, and sent them outside to play. He poked the short sapling through the wheelbarrow leg openings, and used cord to tie each end to a leg. He called the children in before dark and put them to bed; he soon followed.

He left the shack early again on Wednesday morning, and pushed the wheelbarrow with the longer sapling resting on it down the shack path almost to the road. Then he walked to the stable and told Sampson how he planned to pull the wheelbarrow.

John visited the crews and returned to his shack; he left the milk and reminded the children he had to go on to Inverness to shop for Ron's group. He came back and tried to catch a young rooster to cook for lunch. When he couldn't catch one for lunch, he waited until the chickens went in their house, to catch one for supper. The delay made the evening meal late, but he used the time to pile up more rocks down by the stream.

He checked often during the next few weeks to learn Stan's fireplace building procedures, and verified in a separate concern that each crew had young roosters to propagate their chicken flock for next year. He used his wheelbarrow towing equipment to move the wheelbarrow eastward a couple times; he continued to pile up rocks on the stream bank at home, tried to entertain the children daily, worked on school plans, and bought two foot sections of stove pipe to top out the flue for each of the four fireplaces.

Ron said his people finished with the wheelbarrow on a Tuesday in August. John responded, "That's great Ron. I'll take it on to my shack and will keep it there when I'm done with it, but if your crew or any of the others want it, let me know, and I'll bring it."

He pulled the wheelbarrow to his shack and wanted to use it immediately, but had to check in his horse and go to Inverness to shop for Ike's group. He cooked lunch after he returned home, and as soon as the children finished eating, he used the wheelbarrow to haul rocks and pile them up behind the shack. He worked until nearly dark, and then left the wheelbarrow behind the shack with the rocks.

Kenzie suggested, "Wouldn't it be easier to put the rocks by the side of the shack closest to the stream?"

"Yes, it would be easier. But I don't want your Uncle Eric to see the rocks and to take them, or to be upset about us cutting a hole in the floor of his shack."

"Uncle Eric hasn't been up here since the day you got mad at him."

"Yes, but if he sees rocks he might come up here to check. If he comes up here when I'm gone, you know what to do, don't you?"

Erroll answered, "Yes, we go inside, put the board across the door, go out the back door, and run away."

"Good. Is that what you would have said, Kenzie?"

"Yes, Poppa."

"Great. I hope it never comes to that, but do it if somebody you don't know or if Uncle Eric comes up here."

John hauled rocks every afternoon except Sunday, and piled up a big stack behind the shack by the end of August. He talked to Kenzie and Erroll when he got back from the stable on Thursday. "I thought we could start school today, because it's September, but now I think we should finish the fireplace before we start school. If we don't finish the fireplace by winter, we'll be cold in here. Are you willing to wait for school?"

"You said we could start in September." Kenzie pouted.

"I did say that a long time ago, but you didn't want to do it here. You wanted friends."

"If I can't have friends, I want to do it here."

"What about you Erroll, are you willing to wait?"

"I guess so. I don't know what school is anyway."

"We'll find out soon enough, but I think we could use most of September to make our fireplace. We can work super hard on school when that's done."

Kenzie continued to pout. "Work? I want to have fun at school."

"Work can be fun, and it won't have to seem like work. And besides, when cold weather comes and we have a fireplace, we can cook inside."

Kenzie frowned, but went along with it. "We can do the fireplace first if we have to."

"Great. Do you want to help?"

Erroll sighed. "Yes."

Kenzie followed Erroll's answer with, "No."

"You don't have to help, Kenzie. Do you want to go with me to the stream to get a bucket of water?"

"Yes."

"Can I go too, Poppa?"

"Sure you can, Erroll."

They all went to the stream for about a quarter-full bucket of water. John took the shovel behind the shack, shoveled dirt into the bucket, and stirred it with a stick to a thick mud mixture. He carried the bucket inside and went back for a rock. When he came inside with the rock, he found Erroll and Kenzie with their hands in the bucket of mud. He glared for an instant, and then grinned. "Feels pretty good, doesn't it?"

John had the children put a layer of mud down on the rocks already in the hole in the floor, in a suitable place to set the first rock of the fireplace, even though he could have done it faster. The children helped until they tired of it, and then John suggested they go out and play. The fireplace went up slowly over the next two weeks, but John finished it on Saturday, September 17. He completed his fireplace last, so when he finished his, all four shacks had a fireplace.

He talked to the children about school when he finished the fireplace. "Today's Saturday, and we can start school on Monday. Is that all right with you?"

"I guess so." Erroll didn't show outward excitement about school, but Kenzie did.

"Yippee!" She ran outside and did a cartwheel.

John talked about school again Sunday when he returned to the shack from the stable. "Monday I have to go into Inverness, like I always do on Mondays, to shop for Art's crew. But we can eat right after I come home, and then we can start school. After we do school an hour, I'll take the ax into the woods to cut limbs off down trees, as a start toward a winter wood supply. I'll do that for only an hour, and then we can have another hour of school, before we build a fire and prepare to eat again. We'll probably do a schedule like that every day except Sunday, until the weather gets too bad to cut wood. Are you fine with that?"

Kenzie responded, "Why can't we have school all day?"

"Well, first because I have to check the herds for Uncle Eric. Next, because you might tire of school anyway after an hour, and finally because we need more wood than we have and we must get it before bad weather begins."

Erroll didn't show interest, but returned to John's original question, and replied with a bored voice, "Yeah. I'm all right with it."

Kenzie added, "Me too."

John read from the Bible to the children, and then sent them out to play, while he cooked the late noon meal. He went out to play hide and seek with them after they finished eating and before he stopped to cook the evening meal.

They began school on Monday after John returned from Inverness. He introduced the children to pencils, paper, and the alphabet; the children learned to make the letters over the next few weeks, and even to print their names. He varied the lesson plans and maintained their enthusiasm more than a month. But a banging noise on the door overshadowed whatever excitement John built for school. He made a fire in the fireplace during a little cold snap in November, mostly to prove he could do it. The banging occurred early the next morning, and it awakened the children.

John opened the door to see his boss, who yelled, "What's this smoke I see coming out of a chimney?"

"I told you to never again come to this shack, Eric."

"It's my shack and I'll come to it when I please. And you're to call me Mr. McCarty."

"You may call yourself Beelzebub if it makes you happy. What you may not do—not now, not ever—is come to this shack."

The boss's face became redder and his voice louder. "I won't have fire in my shack. You can burn up yourself and your snot noses if you want to, but I won't have you setting fire to my chickens."

John's face also grew a bit rosier. "Goodbye, Eric." He slammed the shack door in his boss's face.

Chapter 14

1887 – 1900

John heard his boss scream through the door, "If you like fire so much, wait until I have a wagon load of wood stacked agin your shack in the middle of the night, and set it afire myself. If you run out the door, I'll shoot you and those two snot-noses."

John didn't reply. He heard a horse depart, looked through a crack at the edge of the door, and saw his boss ride back toward the mansion. He spoke softly to the children. "Wow. Uncle Eric talks crazy sometimes, doesn't he?"

Kenzie cried and asked, "Why doesn't Uncle Eric like us?"

"I don't think it's really you, or you and Erroll he doesn't like. It's me."

"Will Uncle Eric shoot us?"

"I'm sure he won't Erroll. But we have to think about it as something he might possibly try to do. I think you should both always go with me to visit the herds, to the stable, and to Inverness, for a long while. I think you two shouldn't be here when I'm not."

"I don't wanta be here if Uncle Eric comes to shoot us, Poppa. I'll go with you. You too, Kenzie?"

Kenzie didn't interrupt her cries, but merely nodded yes.

John tried to comfort Kenzie, and invited both children to put their coats on and go with him to the garden, before they walked to the stable. They went, and they picked the remainder of the green beans, the navy beans, and every tomato with red on it. They had dug the potatoes and stored them under the foot of Kenzie's bed, back in September.

They opened the chicken house door before they went inside with the garden products, and then all walked to the stable, where Sampson commented, "Hey, I see you have your children with you. Is this a special day for them?"

"No, the boss threatened to burn—"

Sampson held up his hand. "Don't tell me about it. Nothing good can come from it if I know."

John saddled a horse, helped Erroll and Kenzie climb a pen fence, stuck a foot in the stirrup and swung his other leg over, then helped the children off the fence and on the horse behind him. "Hold on tight. We'll go nice and slow, but we'll go a long ways."

They approached the herds at a slow walk. John helped the children off the horse at each stop to give them a break, and then helped them back on. They started about an hour late, moved slowly, and John took time to explain to each crew.

Ron began the conversation at the Beauty Firth Beauties crew. "Hi John. Who ye got with ye?"

"My pride and joys, Ron. We talked about my son Erroll and my daughter Kenzie, and here they are. Kenzie and Erroll, this is Ron. This is Bob, and this is Orville."

All three men smiled, and Ron shook Erroll's and Kenzie's hands as well. He said, "Your paw's talked about ye, and we're really glad t' finally meet ye." Ron grinned and continued, "We always think your paw's truthful, but it's good ye're 'ere t' prove 'e is. Ye come back as often as ye can."

Neither Erroll nor Kenzie answered, but John did. "I think they'll be with me every day for a while. Something pretty bad happened to us this morning. The boss saw smoke from our fireplace, didn't like it, and threatened to burn our shack with us in it, so I don't want to leave the children alone there. I'm already in a fight with him, at least a word fight, and it might be better if you don't use your fireplace until we see how my fight turns out. I plan to win, and believe me, I won't sell you out. Another thing I won't do is leave Kenzie and Erroll there under his nose."

Orville looked especially combative as John spoke, and he responded first. "We'll take care of Erroll and Kenzie if you leave them here while you visit the other herds. McCarty'll have to step over my dead body to get to them."

John looked at Erroll and Kenzie, but Kenzie gave her opinion before he could ask. "We want to go with you, Poppa."

Orville spoke up again. "I understand if they don't want to stay here. But if they ever change their mind, I won't change mine. I'll protect them with my life. Do you think you should carry a rifle? You can borrow ours if you want it."

"No, I don't want to get into a shooting match with the boss. I didn't see a gun this morning, and don't think he had one. I'm younger, taller, and stronger than he is, and I'll be quick to move his nose around to the side of his face if he messes with my children. Still, I recommend you wait to start a fire in the fireplace."

Ron dissented. "We'll start a fire t'night if it's cool enough. Ah don't think McCarty wants t' fight us all."

"We need to go, but be careful." John and the children walked back to the horse, climbed on top, and continued west.

Similar conversations occurred at the other two herds with an added detail at the Hummer Bunch. John told Art, "In a way I'm pleased you support me, but in another way, I really do think you should wait to use the fireplace until you see what happens to us. I intend to visit you every day as always, but if someday I don't, you'll know there's trouble."

Stan normally didn't initiate a conversation with John, but this time he did. "If we think ye're more'n a' hour late, we're gonna 'ead east. And Ah'll bet unless guys at th' Middle Valley 'erd know why ye're late, they'll go with us. Ah'll bet afore th' day's done ye'll have nine men at your shack, an' if ye're there dead, it won't be more'n a few minutes afore McCarty'll 'ave nine men tearin' down 'is mansion t' get at 'im."

John responded mostly to Stan, but also to Art and Thomas. "I don't think it will ever go that far, but if it does, it's my fight and not yours. If the boss doesn't allow fireplaces, you'll be ahead to quit, rather than die in my fight. But we need to go."

John and the children walked to the horse, mounted up, and rode east. The horse took only a few steps, and Kenzie asked, "Will we all die?"

"No, Kenzie, I don't expect anybody to die over a fireplace. Uncle Eric talks crazy and the men sound too much wrought up, but I hope it's already over. You're with me today only as a 'just-in-case' precaution. I can handle Uncle Eric if he bothers us again, and he won't kill anyone."

The children didn't talk for most of the remainder of the return trip, but complained about fatigue toward the end of the ride. John heard happy comments when he let them off the horse while he stopped to milk the tall cow, but he didn't let them off when they left the milk at the shack. They all walked from the stable to Inverness before they could turn back to the shack.

The children claimed to be exhausted when they entered the shack. John asked, "Do you think we can skip school today?"

Kenzie answered for both. "I usually like school, but I'm too tired for it today. We haven't had a nap for a long time, but can we do it today?"

"Of course, Kenzie. Do you want a nap Erroll?"

"I don't know if I'll go to sleep, but it sure will feel good to lay down."

"You children do that and I'll be quiet or be outside, but I won't leave you alone here."

The children slept until John awakened them for their evening meal. They ate, and then went outside to play, but soon came back in to check on bedtime. He put them to bed a half hour early. John left the shack door open because of his boss's threat to burn it in the night;

he tried and failed to stay awake, but Sampson awakened him. "I usually don't talk about Mr. McCarty's business, but I have a wagonload of wood out here he ordered me to stack against your cabin. I don't know if he'll be down later tonight or not."

"Thanks for warning me Sampson. I won't tell the boss we talked."

Sampson unloaded the wood, but placed all of it at the east side of the shack, and none in front of the door. He went back east, and John re-stacked the wood about fifteen yards behind the shack, near his other wood. He could heat the shack all winter with it if the boss would leave it alone. He remained awake the rest of the night to wait for the boss, but he didn't come.

John woke Kenzie and Erroll the next morning, and didn't mention the wood. They ate their usual egg breakfast and walked to the stable, where John talked briefly with Sampson. "Just a bit of information, Sampson. We had a quiet night last night."

"I don't need to know about that. Which horse do you want?"

"I think I'll ask Kenzie to choose. Do you want to go to the back of the stable and look at horses, Kenzie?"

"Can we have the same one we had yesterday?"

Sampson exclaimed, "Sure you can! I'll get him."

John saddled the horse. The entire family straddled his back, and they rode west. They made better time than the day before, and John told the crews no trouble happened during the night. When they returned and came near their shack, however, they saw the boss's horse tied to a tree by the road, and the boss sat on the ground by the tree. John tried to ignore the boss and take the milk to the shack.

The boss stepped in front of his horse and forced him to stop. "What'd you think of the wood I sent down here last night?"

"It might be real."

"You better believe it's real. What'd you do with it?"

John smirked. "Burned it all in the fireplace."

"You're a liar."

John helped Kenzie and Erroll down off the horse and told them to walk to the stable. He said he'd meet them there. Then he turned back toward his boss. "Wood's a valuable commodity. When can you bring more?"

"Poke fun all you want. You won't think it's fun when I set it afire."

"Eric, you absolutely must stop talking crazy. If anybody hears you, they'll think you truly are crazy."

"That's Mr. McCarty to you, you scum."

"You're whatever I want to call you, Eric. If you bother me about it I'll make sure people know how crazy you really are."

"I should shoot you right now."

"You're talking crazy again, Eric. But you'd better never go near that shack."

"You don't believe I'll do it?"

"I'll go now, Eric." John took a big drink of milk and threw the remainder near, but not on, his boss. "My children are almost to the stable and I don't want them there when I'm not."

"I'll go ahead of you and wring their necks."

John slipped the bridle off his boss's horse and slapped the horse on the rump. "I don't think you'll go ahead of me, and if I see you move closer to the shack, I'll come back here and wallop you." John turned his horse, galloped toward the stable for only a few seconds, then stopped, and looked backward at his boss. His boss walked toward the stable too, yelling with every step, but when he got close enough to throw a clod, John went on to the stable. He took the children inside and waited there, either until he could have it out with the boss, or until he walked past the stable. The latter happened. John and the children walked to Inverness much earlier than they did on Monday.

Tuesday was the day to buy for Ike's group, and they only had to visit the grocery store that day for Ike. They shopped, and then turned back toward home. John informed the children, "We won't have milk when we get back to the shack, because I poured it on the ground beside your Uncle Eric."

Neither child responded to John about the milk, but Erroll asked, "Is Uncle Eric crazy?"

"I don't know, Erroll, but sometimes he acts as if he is. I think he's harmless, but we don't want to provoke him if we don't have to." They walked in silence a few steps, and John spoke again. "What do you think about a one week school vacation? We can start again on Monday."

Kenzie shook her head. "We already didn't do anything yesterday, and I'm not tired today."

Erroll added, "Me neither."

John laughed. "I don't know if I can stay awake, but I don't want to stop you from learning. If you want school, school we'll have."

They returned to their shack, where John started a fire and cooked the late noon meal. They did their usual hour of school followed by an hour off, and another hour of school before the evening meal. The children continued to ride with John and to walk with him to Inverness, as well as to learn in school. Cold weather came. John used the fireplace regularly, and argued with his boss about it only one more time.

The argument happened at the stable in front of Sampson in late November. The boss waited there for John and the children to return their horse, and when they did, he asked, "When will you bring the wood back?"

"What wood? Back where?"

"You know what wood."

"You mean the wood you had delivered and stacked against the shack?"

"That would be it."

"You brought it. You're free to send somebody after it if you want it, provided you don't come near the shack. You should send somebody right away if you want it, because I burned some of it last night, and will burn more every night until it's gone."

"That's right, bluster on. You're gonna wake up dead one of these days."

"You're talking crazy again Eric. Maybe you're drunk. Maybe you ought to stagger up to your mansion and sleep it off."

Eric stomped out the stable door, and Sampson tried to offer advice to John. "He's right you know."

"About what?"

"About you waking up dead one of these days. He can see to it."

"Don't tell me he scared you too. He won't get past the talking stage."

"Don't be so sure."

"What are you talking about Sampson?"

"If you don't know, I can't explain it."

"You already said that to me. What do you mean by it?"

"I mean exactly what I said. You need to go now."

John looked around and replied, "You're right. Come on children." They didn't have to go to Inverness that day, so they walked back to their shack.

John took each person's pay with him on Friday, payday, and also asked if the boss hassled anybody about a fireplace. The leader of each group answered he hadn't seen the boss for weeks.

They returned the horse to the stable when they returned from their ride, and John told the children, "We get to shop for ourselves today. I saved money all summer, and we can buy new shoes and coats for all of us, plus a food treat. We can afford a little more food than usual this week, but we need real food, not candy."

Kenzie described coat details she wanted, but John stopped her. "We'll buy something the store has, and not the most expensive thing. We might as well wait until we go in the store to see what we can choose from. What kind of food do you want?"

Kenzie answered, "Bread."

Erroll, "Meat."

John suggested they wait to decide about food too, until they saw the available choices. They all chose a coat—a warm one after some coaching—and all chose warm, lace-up shoes. Kenzie continued to want bread and Erroll meat, so they bought two loaves of bread and some summer sausage. The children wanted to wear their new coats, and John allowed them to do it, although the sun warmed them that day.

The weather turned cold in early December, and the children wore their coats at night, though John kept a fire. Ron said the winter featured more snow and cold than normal, but John claimed he routinely saw worse in Rochester. The herdsmen all stayed through the winter, maybe partly because they had fireplaces, and partly because they could arrange with John to buy food and clothing they wanted.

The children wanted to stay in the shack by the fireplace one cold January morning, and Kenzie made the case. "We'll be awful cold on the horse. Uncle Eric won't burn the shack down. We aren't scared of him, and we can stay home while you go out and ride the horse, right Erroll?"

"Right."

"You're probably both right, but I think we must take every precaution on the off chance Uncle Eric will try something when I'm not here."

Erroll countered, "You showed us how to get out the back. We can do that and Uncle Eric will never catch us."

"We have snow all around the shack, so he can follow your tracks however long it takes to catch up to you."

Kenzie inquired, "What if there's a day when there's no snow on the ground? We'll be all right that day won't we?"

"Uncle Eric won't mess with me, because he knows I can swing him around like I have a snake by the tail. But he knows he can do the same to you, and I think it's too much risk."

Kenzie tried another tactic. "Poppa, you're a stick-in-the-mud."

"Maybe I am, but I'd rather be stuck in the mud and have you, than take a chance and not have you. You can stay with Ron and his group if you prefer. You'll be as safe with them as you'll be with me."

Kenzie appeared to consider it until Erroll uttered a loud, "No!"

"It's settled then. We need to walk down to the stable, and it's time to go."

The children rode with John that day, and every day until they were sixteen years old. They argued about it often, but he never gave in. He continued to worry even after they grew up, but he allowed them to stay home starting on Kenzie's sixteenth birthday. She took over most of the cooking soon after, and Erroll the wood gathering. John needed the help, even at fifty years old, because his years weighed heavily. He suffered from arthritis and sometimes asked Erroll to ride in his place. The herdsmen changed too. Only Stan and Ed remained from the crews John supervised during his first year. The other herdsmen either retired or moved on to better jobs, aided by letters of reference from John.

The Patersons checked books out often from the Inverness Public Library, and John continued to instruct the children until they completed twelve years of school in the spring of 1900.

John told off his boss occasionally during all the time until the children finished their school, but changed his life then in a major way. He retired and turned supervision of the crews entirely over to Erroll. His arthritis worsened, and hurt him especially during cold or wet times. He no longer stood up to his former boss, but Erroll sometimes confronted the boss to defend John or the cattle crews.

Erroll's first argument with the boss occurred in the fall of 1900, when he happened to meet him in the stable. "Hey boss, there's something I want to talk to you about."

"Well whoopee-doo. Do you think I care?"

"Yeah, I think you should."

"What's it about?"

"It's about Poppa. His arthritis bothers him more in cold weather and if you can add some insulation to the shack and cover—"

The boss didn't allow Erroll to finish. "Your 'Poppa' is lucky I didn't shoot him years ago. I don't give a rip if his arthritis hurts or not, and in fact, I hope it does."

"If that's how you wanta be, I'll take you to court about it."

"Go ahead. You're a foreigner and I'm a citizen. You'll lose."

Erroll turned, stomped out of the stable leading his horse, and rode away, but the same evening he spoke to his father. "I think it's time for Kenzie and me to become Scottish citizens. Do you agree?"

John said, "My dream remains to take you both back to New York. I know I can't do it now, but will you try to go someday, and take Kenzie with you? If you do, then Scottish citizenship won't matter."

"Poppa, you know we can never afford to go. The boss paid you regularly but never gave you a raise. Not only did he not give me a raise, he misses a week here and there. We don't have money for it, we'll never have enough, and we don't remember anything about New York anyway."

"Don't forget about going back, but I support whatever you do in the meantime. There's an office in Inverness where you can start the citizenship process, right behind the grocery

Chapter 15

1900 – 1902

Erroll soon stopped at the United Kingdom Border Agency's field office in Inverness to ask questions about how to be a Scottish citizen, and told John what he learned when he returned to the shack. "We're fine on everything, except we have to take a test. The people at the office told me we can enroll in a night class to prepare. That means you'll be alone here at night sometimes, Poppa. Is that all right with you?"

"I'll always hope you can go back to New York, but will support your efforts to achieve citizenship here. You talk about 'we' can take a class and say I'll be alone. Do you mean Kenzie will take the class too?"

"I haven't talked to her, but I hope she will. Will you Kenzie?"

Kenzie knotted a thread on an unfinished coat. "Will I what?"

"Will you take a class to learn how to pass the test to become a Scottish citizen?"

"Why?"

"We'll be equal under the law to everybody else around here if we're Scottish citizens."

"Why do we care about the law?"

"Maybe we don't care today, but we might wanta take somebody to court . . . perhaps . . . someday."

Kenzie's eyes switched from Erroll back to her sewing. "Like who?"

"Well, like . . . maybe like Eric McCarty . . . maybe. I don't know."

Kenzie's eyes jumped away from the coat and back toward Erroll. "Eric McCarty? What could be dumber than to take Eric McCarty to court? Do you want us in jail?"

John interjected, "Kenzie's correct, Erroll. You don't want to mess with the McCartys often, and when you do, you want to be as far away from the law as you can."

Erroll tried again. "Maybe you're both right. Maybe we don't want to take anybody to court, but it will still be good to be the same as everybody else around here. You think, Kenzie?"

"Yes, I'll do it someday, if you want to. We don't have to do it today, do we?"

"No, we might walk up to the office tomorrow after I check the herds, and find out when we can begin. Are you game for that?"

"Tomorrow is someday? I suppose it is. I'll try to be ready to go."

Erroll had to buy for the Beauty Firth Beauties crew the next day, but he stopped at the shack for Kenzie, they walked the horse to the stable, and then walked to the Border Agency office.

The lady behind the counter in the office recognized Erroll. "I know you; you're John Paterson's boy. What's your first name?"

"Erroll. We're here to find out when we can take the class to prepare us for the citizenship test." The lady wrote in a book.

"And what's your wife's name?" Kenzie grinned, and Erroll frowned.

"She's not my wife, she's my sister."

"Oh, I'm sorry for the mistake. What's her name?"

"Kenzie Cox."

"She's your sister?"

"Yes."

"Why isn't her name Paterson?" Kenzie grinned again and Erroll frowned again.

"Well, she's not really my sister, but she lives with Poppa and me." Kenzie embarked on an extended laughing fit.

The lady glared mostly at Kenzie, but also at Erroll. She wrote again in the book. "I don't see what's so funny about it. Her momma must be really proud. Will you both take the test?"

Erroll spoke quickly. "You can take it and—I mean—yes, we will. For sure we will. When can we start the class?"

"It will be a couple months before another class begins."

"That's all right. When will it begin?"

"Wait here a moment." The lady sighed, struggled up from her chair, went to the back of the room, and engaged in a long whispered conversation with a man seated at a desk there. Both shot disapproving looks at Kenzie, who continued to giggle.

The lady came back, fell into her chair, wrote in the book again, and motioned Erroll to lean close. "The class will begin in several months, on June 4. Both you and Miss Cox may enroll. You each need to sign up and pay an enrollment fee not later than that day."

"Thank you, we'll do it. How much will—?"

"I hope Miss Cox can be more serious if she comes back here."

Erroll frowned again. He looked at Kenzie, frowned more, unsuccessfully tried to catch her eye, and replied, "She'll be serious if she cares to be, but not unless. Good day." He turned abruptly. He and Kenzie left the office.

Erroll tried to open a new subject. "We need to—"

Kenzie interrupted. "Do you know what I think?" She giggled more.

"How can I know what you think?"

"I mean, do you know what I think the lady in the office thought?"

"If I did know what she thought, I wouldn't want to talk about it." Kenzie giggled until she was out of breath. Erroll went on, "We need to go to the clothing store to buy hats for the guys at the first herd, then by the grocery to get potatoes and bread for them." Kenzie broke into frequent giggles as they shopped, and continued as they walked home. Erroll didn't understand. "Why aren't you mad at the lady in the Border Agency office? Why do you just laugh at her?"

"Why Erroll, whatever are you talking about?" Erroll didn't answer.

Kenzie continued to laugh even after she and Erroll returned to the shack, so much that John mentioned it to her. "You two apparently enjoyed your walk."

Kenzie glanced quickly in Erroll's direction and then looked away. "I did. I'm not sure about Erroll, but you can ask him." She laughed again.

Kenzie sometimes rode along with Erroll to visit the crews, and she asked if she could do it the morning after the office visit. Erroll answered, "Sure, it will make the trip fun."

They walked to the stable together. Sampson brought a horse for them and commented, "You two look happy this morning. What's going on?"

Kenzie drew a finger over her lips to signal she would not talk, so Erroll replied, "Nothing's going on. We're on our way to visit the crews, that's all."

Sampson smiled. "Aye, right. That's all. I'll see you when you come back." He continued to smile.

Erroll saddled the horse and he and Kenzie rode west. Kenzie held tight and caused Erroll to protest, "You're drivin' me crazy. Can you slide back a little?"

"Erroll, I'm trying to drive you crazy. Don't you understand?"

"Understand what?"

"That we're about to fall in love."

Erroll nearly fell off the horse, and would have, except Kenzie held him on. "About to what?"

"About to fall in love."

"How'd you come up with a lunatic notion like that?"

"Didn't you say I drive you crazy?"

"You took that literally?"

"Yes, and do you think I could do it if you didn't like me as more than a sister?"

Erroll took an unusual interest in the horizon, and studied it for a time. "Maybe, maybe not. If I did, don't you think I'd know about it?"

"I'm not sure you'd know about it if your head fell off." Kenzie slipped into more laughter.

"All right, let's say I might someday like you as more than a sister. What would we do about it?" Erroll didn't laugh out loud, but did grin slightly.

Kenzie didn't answer for a moment. "Out of respect for Poppa, we have to control it. We can talk about it when he's not around, but he sees us as sister and brother, and he'll never understand."

"If you're right about the love thing I don't think we can hide it from him. He's not as dumb as you think."

"Erroll, he is. He's old. What can he know about us?"

"Everything, Kenzie. He changed our diapers, remember?"

"No, I don't remember and you don't either. But that has nothing to do with anything, Erroll. We know he won't approve, even if he knows."

"You might be right, and about the love deal too. If you want to go with me and drive me crazy every day, go right ahead. But in the shack around Poppa, you'll have to act normal . . . if you can."

"Erroll! What a thing to say!"

Erroll and Kenzie completed their visits to the crews, took the horse back to the stable, and walked to the shack. Erroll asked, "Is it because of us you laughed so much at the lady in the Border Agency office?"

"Erroll, I'm shocked! I laughed because you didn't know what the lady at the counter could see plain as day. You were the funny one."

They walked along in silence for a few steps. Erroll managed to say, "Oh." He didn't speak further until they returned to the shack.

The next two years went by, much like all the others. Kenzie and Erroll passed their tests and added UK citizenship to their American. They made joint trips to visit crews, took long walks in the woods, and Erroll had only two spats with the boss. The boss ignored most of Erroll's paydays and Erroll put up with it, but he missed a payday for the crews in late winter of 1901, and Erroll determined he wouldn't tolerate it. He left a note with Sampson, as John did in earlier years, and asked for a meeting.

The boss showed up at the stable in a few days. Erroll walked to the stable alone that day, but didn't shrink from the argument. "How come you didn't pay the crews last Friday?"

"Because I didn't feel like paying them."

"Will it be satisfactory if they don't feel like working for you some day?"

"Sure. I'll fire them, but they don't have to work for me if they don't want to."

"You paid them reliably for several years, most of them since they first began to work here. What am I supposed to tell them if you stop?"

"Tell 'em anything you want. Tell 'em you fed their pay to the cows. Tell 'em a big wind—tell 'em anything, but don't let me hear about it."

Erroll's face turned red and his voice grew loud. "You'll hear about it every day until you pay them. You'll hear, and everybody this side of the firth will hear, until you pay them."

"What do I care? What will you do about it? I can swat you like a fly—and your paw, too. I can fire you too, you know."

"Leave Poppa out of this. If I can't represent you as a reliable employer to the men, then you won't have to fire me. I'll quit."

"I hardly think so. Where will you go?"

"Straight to court. You can't wriggle out of your debt to these men."

"You're a foreigner and I'm a citizen. You'll lose."

Erroll moved closer until his chin almost touched the boss's nose. "Try me. I want that pay this morning."

"I don't have it on me."

"I got all day. I'll wait here."

"I'll fire you if this happens one more time."

"Great. Bring the money."

The boss glared at Erroll and left the stable. Sampson appeared from behind a hayrack and warned, "It's none of my business boy, but you be careful with Mr. McCarty."

Erroll's eyes turned to Sampson, and away from the door the boss used. "Thanks Sampson. I appreciate your concern, but the boss'll dish out guff to anybody willing to take it, and I'm not willing." Sampson shook his head and went behind the hay rack again.

Erroll waited several minutes before the boss came with the men's pay, but he did eventually come. Erroll didn't thank him or comment in any way. He merely counted the money, mounted his horse, and rode out to deliver the pay.

John awoke with a bad cough one morning about a year after Erroll clashed with the boss over pay. Kenzie said the cough could be pneumonia, so Erroll didn't wait for the normal message/stable meeting, but went directly to the mansion early, and knocked on a door. A man opened the door after he knocked several minutes. "Yes?"

"I'm Erroll Paterson. I wanta see McCarty."

The man looked shocked. "Who?"

"Mr. McCarty."

"I'm afraid that won't be possible, Sir. Mr. McCarty is taking his breakfast now, and must not be disturbed."

"If you won't disturb him, I'll do it." Erroll moved to go around the man.

The man rang a bell similar to a school bell, and two more men showed up. The man continued, "You were saying?"

"I'm saying I'll disturb McCarty if you won't. Get out of my way."

The three men stepped closer together to completely block the door opening, and the first man said softly, "You'd better go now, Sir."

Erroll picked up a rock and broke the glass in a nearby window. All three men's jaws slackened. "If you won't let me go in the door, I'll go through the window, but I intend to see McCarty."

One of the recent arrivals shook his entire body and commanded, "Keep calm. I'll ask Mr. McCarty if he'll see you." The man walked rapidly toward mansion interior.

Erroll called after him, "He'd better come to me unless he wants me to go to him." He waited for something to happen.

Something did happen after a couple minutes; the boss came to the door and yelled, "Don't you ever come to my mansion again. I live here and you're to show proper respect."

"There'll be time for respect later. Poppa's got pneumonia, and I want you to send your coach down to the shack to take him into town to Doc McWilliston."

"Are you suggesting to me what I do with my coach?" The boss stressed the words 'me' and 'my', and pointed to his chest as he said them.

"No, I'm telling you."

"And who do you think will pay for all that?"

"You will."

"What?"

"You will. You kept Poppa poor all his life. He can't afford to leave, and he can't afford to stay. You're the guy to take him to the doctor and to pay for it, so hop to it."

"Not today, and not ever." The boss turned and started to walk away.

Erroll slammed his hand against the door casing. "You want me to tell everybody how crazy you are?"

The boss turned and came back. "You watch your step you scum."

"I'll not watch anything except your carriage take Poppa to the doctor."

"You want to ride in the carriage with your 'Poppa'?"

Erroll ignored the sarcasm in the boss's word 'Poppa', and said, "Sure do."

"Go to your shack. I'll send the carriage sometime this morning."

Chapter 16

1902 - 1904

Erroll hurried back to the shack. He alerted Kenzie and John, and he and Kenzie helped John put on his coat and hat. They helped John climb into the carriage when it showed up, helped him settle into it, and waited to go.

The driver took exception to Kenzie. "Mr. McCarty telt me t' take John an' Erroll. 'E didn't say nothin' 'bout Kenzie."

Erroll slammed his hand again. "She's going. Now you go."

The liveryman clucked to the horses and went to Inverness; he pulled up in front of Dr. McWilliston's office, where Kenzie and Erroll helped John out of the carriage, and Erroll directed the liveryman, "Wait for us. I don't know how long we'll be."

The liveryman opened his mouth to protest, but the doctor had already opened the door to Kenzie's knock. The liveryman shrugged and waited. Erroll held the door and supported John, while Kenzie entered the office. Before the doctor could ask, she reported that her Poppa—John Paterson—stood outside with pneumonia.

Dr. McWilliston put a stethoscope on John's back and chest. He maintained his habitual gloomy look, but announced, "Mr. Paterson has only a bad cold."

Erroll's shoulders relaxed. He appeared to digest the report a moment and then exclaimed, "That's great news! What should we do for him?"

"Give him time. Let him rest, give him plenty of water, and he'll get well on his own."

Kenzie beamed and helped John with his coat. "Oh thank you, doctor. You can't know how relieved we are."

The doctor broke in, "What about payment?"

Erroll responded, "Put it on Eric McCarty's bill."

"He'll never pay it."

Erroll raised his voice slightly. "He'd better. If he doesn't, let me know, and I'll make him do it."

Dr. McWilliston snorted and muttered, but the Patersons went outside and into the carriage. Erroll stuck his head out the door and yelled, "Take us home." The liveryman took them.

Erroll knocked on Dr. McWilliston's office door during his regular Monday trip to Inverness a little over a week later, and when the doctor opened it he inquired, "Did McCarty ever pay you?"

"'Course not."

"Did you bill him yet?"

"I sent my son over the same day you were here. He knows how much he owes, but he'll never pay."

"Yes he will. Give me another week to make him do it."

Dr. McWilliston's usual somber countenance remained, he mumbled under his breath, and slammed the door.

Erroll wrote a note to ask the boss to meet him in the stable on Tuesday, when he went back past there on his way to the shack. The boss didn't show up Tuesday, but did Wednesday, and asked, "What's this about now?"

"About Dr. McWilliston's bill."

"That's not my bill."

"I expect you to pay it today."

"Expect all you want, but it's not my bill."

"We've already been through all that. Pay it today."

"So if you get a hangnail tonight, will you want me to pay for that too?"

"Pay what you owe today. Bye." Erroll left the stable with his boss still sputtering. He checked back with Dr. McWilliston the following Monday, and the doctor reported the bill paid.

All during the first years of the 1900's, Erroll and Kenzie became more and more aware of their love for each other. They told each other often, but also told each other John would feel like an intruder in their home if they married. Kenzie changed her mind when the 1903-1904 winter began, however, and pushed her view. "I think we should set a date and tell Poppa after my birthday in January."

"How about if we wait until the Tiny Kirk wagon comes by in the early summer to set a date and tell him?"

"What's special about the wagon?"

"What's special about your birthday?"

"Maybe nothing. I can wait for the wagon if you can."

"I don't want to wait either, Kenzie, but Poppa's so weak now. I hate to put any more on him than winter already does. Maybe he'll be stronger when spring comes."

"Well, I suppose I can go with that. He has to know sometime, but if you think winter's the wrong time, I—"

"Thanks, Kenzie. I know you love Poppa as much as I do. Spring's a lot longer to wait, but I think spring's a better time."

Kenzie and Erroll didn't tell John they intended to marry, and he died in his sleep on Monday, February 15, 1904, a month and a day after Kenzie's twenty-second birthday. Kenzie woke up first that morning and discovered him. She screamed and awakened Erroll. "What is it Kenzie?"

"Poppa! He's dead!"

"What?"

"He's dead."

"How do you know?"

"You're right there beside him. Look."

Erroll looked. He didn't ask for time off, but no one visited the crews for the first time since the Patersons came to Scotland back in 1887. They buried John down by the stream. Erroll never read the Bible before they buried John, but he went back to the shack afterward, searched until he found John's Bible, returned to the grave, and read

Psalm twenty-three aloud. Then he worked most of the day to carry rocks to make a large and impressive monument.

Kenzie didn't carry rocks, but she talked to Erroll while he carried. "We can't live together without Poppa, because we're not married. Nobody'd understand that, not even us."

"Maybe I can sleep in the stable a few months, or maybe we ought to move our wedding day up a little."

"That's a wonderful idea. How about tomorrow?"

"Tomorrow? That's moving it up a lot."

"How long do you want to sleep in the stable?"

"Not even one night, but at the same time, I don't think we should enjoy Poppa's death for any reason."

"That's dumb, Erroll. Poppa worked his whole life to make us happy, and he doesn't want us to be miserable because of him. I only regret he didn't live to see us married."

"I'm not sure about your regret, but I for sure need to see the crews tomorrow, to explain why I didn't come today." Erroll stopped, but then went on. "How about if you walk into Inverness in the morning, to talk to the pastor at Tiny Kirk, and we walk back there in the afternoon to get married? I'll need to shop afterward for two crews, because I missed today."

"I don't care if you have to work. I just want to be able to live with you, to do it with a clear conscience, and to do it in a better way than before. I'll be a perfect wife, and I know you'll be a perfect husband. I'll go into Inverness tomorrow and set it all up."

Sampson chided Erroll when he showed up at the stable near dusk. "You're awful late today, Erroll. You're not about to go out at night are you?"

"No, Sampson. I didn't go today, because Poppa died last night, and we buried him today. Kenzie and I plan to marry tomorrow, but it isn't right for me to sleep in the shack tonight, because we're not married now. Do you have an empty stall I can sleep in?"

"You betcha, Erroll. Nothing better'n your Poppa could've ever happened to Mr. McCarty's cattle crews. The new men don't know him, but he's a legend . . . they've heard about him . . . I'm really sorry, and I know they will be too. But this marrying thing's been coming on for a while. You got my congratulations about that, and my condolences about your Poppa."

Erroll returned to the shack early the next morning. Sampson never told any of the Patersons where he slept, and Erroll didn't find out, because he left before he saw Sampson. He went back to the stable alone after breakfast, saddled a horse, visited the crews, and told everyone about John. Kenzie walked to Tiny Kirk in Inverness, and talked to Pastor MacIntire, who agreed to perform a wedding in the afternoon. Erroll and Kenzie showed up at the kirk at the appointed time and married in their normal work clothes, on February 16, 1904. They shopped for two crews, and went into the bakery across the street from the grocery store on the way back to the shack; they splurged slightly in the bakery, and came out with a store-bought chocolate pie.

They talked as they walked back to the shack, Kenzie first. "Erroll, I'm so excited to actually be a Paterson, but that's only the minor part of it. I'm most excited that I'm a Paterson because I'm married to you." She put extra stress on the last word.

"I'm glad you're a Paterson for exactly the same reason. I love you Kenzie, as I have for more than two years now. I never thought it would happen, but it did in a big way, and I'm glad it did. Do you think you'll go with me to talk to the crews tomorrow?"

"I'm not sure. Did you tell anyone we'd marry today?"

"Only Sampson."

"Then you must tell the crews tomorrow. And you can do it better if I'm not listening."

"I don't know why it matters if you listen. But yes, I must do it tomorrow, and can't not do it. My problem for tomorrow is I want to head out to the crews late and return early."

Kenzie laughed. "That's what I want you to do, too."

"What's for dinner tonight?"

"Is that all you care about?"

"Not on your life. Forget I asked."

"We have pie." She held it aloft.

"That'll do for me. And I'll even save a small piece for you."

"Erroll! I'll cut the pie, and I'll say how much you get. You might not get even one piece!"

Erroll elbowed Kenzie on her side. "Tag. You're it." He ran.

She chased him and caught him when he slowed to look back. She pushed him with one hand as he ran in the middle of the muddy road. They were directly in front of the stable, with Sampson looking on; she didn't drop the pie, and although he went to his knees, he didn't drop the items for the two crews. Sampson chuckled and waved, but neither of the newlyweds looked toward the stable. She allowed him up and tagged him; he chased her all the way to the shack.

Erroll showed up at the stable the next morning only a half hour later than he normally did. He checked out a horse and went to see the Beauty Firth Beauties crew.

He greeted Ted, current crew leader, and after their usual banter, Ted observed, "The best grass is in the upper valley, but it's covered with snow, so we had to feed hay yesterday afternoon. No problem though, we have plenty."

"Great, Ted. You and your crew do a good job with this herd, but I wanta tell you news that's important to me. Kenzie and I married yesterday."

Ted moved backward a step. "Aren't you and Kenzie brother and sister?"

"Poppa raised us as brother and sister, but we're actually no relation."

"John must have been crazy to bring kids to McCarty's estate."

"Poppa didn't do anything crazy in his life, and I couldn't want a better life than he gave us."

"You're right. Congratulations, Erroll. I hope you two will be nothing but happy."

"Thanks, Ted. This is Wednesday, and your day to tell me what you want in Inverness. You have a list with money?"

"Yep. Here's the list and the money. You be careful going to those other herds, you hear?"

"Yeah, yeah." Erroll grinned. "Did you ever see me not be careful?" Erroll mounted his horse, and rode away. He explained to each of the other two groups why he and Kenzie could marry, but still made it back to the shack with milk only a half hour later than his normal time. He dismounted from the horse, took the milk inside, kissed Kenzie, remounted, and rode to the stable.

Sampson ribbed Erroll when he arrived at the stable. "Your pants had a lot of mud on them yesterday. Looks like you got 'em cleaned up, but I tell you one thing, if you want to stay married to that Kenzie, you need to learn to run faster."

Erroll grinned. "You're right about almost everything Sampson, so you're probably right about that too. She's fast, but I bet I can run longer. She'll never escape by running."

Erroll left the horse at the stable, walked to Inverness, shopped for Ted's crew, and walked home. When there, he told Kenzie, "This old shack seems more like home than it ever did before. I look forward to old age with you, right here. The boss hasn't been on our back for a while. Perhaps he mellowed and will get better and better."

"We might get better and better, but we can't count on mellow from that old fellow. He's a so-and-so you know."

Erroll laughed at Kenzie, and declared, "You're nothing but a pessimist."

"Perhaps. You always see only the good, but your vision is terrible! When will you learn mine is better?"

Chapter 17

1904

Kenzie suggested a change inside the shack the first day after she married. "Will you approve if I remove the privacy curtain Poppa put up years ago?"

"Kenzie, I approve of everything you do!" Erroll tried to look shocked.

"Seriously?" She laughed.

"I don't care about the privacy curtain one way or the other. Whatever you do with it is all right with me."

"Good. It'll be gone by dawn."

Erroll waked up earlier on Thursday and arrived at the stable at his regular time, but Sampson stumbled and staggered. "You all right, Sampson?"

"Not really. I think I ate something that doesn't agree with me. I'll get over it." Sampson went back into the stable for a horse, almost made it back to Erroll, lost his grip on the horse's halter, and collapsed on the stable floor.

Erroll didn't take time to tie the horse, but ran a couple steps and put Sampson's head in his lap. Sampson said one word, closed his eyes, and after a moment, said another. He didn't move again. He first said, "small . . . ," then perhaps, "watch."

He continued to hold Sampson for several minutes, but when he remained still, Erroll stood up and tied the horse to a hayrack. He walked toward the east stable door, but traveled only a few steps, before the boss's liveryman entered the stable. "I'm really glad to see you. I think Sampson's dead. He's there on the floor; you might see what you think."

The liveryman went to Sampson, touched him, and agreed. "'E's dead, that's for sure. Were ye 'ere when 'e died?"

"Yes, he fell there where he is, as he brought me that horse." Erroll pointed to the horse.

"Did 'e say anything?"

"Not much. He said a few words, but they didn't seem connected, didn't make sense. Will you tell the boss?"

"The boss don't care 'bout Sampson. 'E's been gripin' 'bout'im lately, but 'e'll need t' get 'nother stable boy. Yeah, Ah'll tell'im."

"Does Sampson have a family to tell?"

"No, nobody. Sampson used t' 'ave 'is own barbershop out on this edge o' Inverness. 'E 'ad a wife and little daughter, but they died when their 'ouse burnt when Sampson was at th' shop. Mr. McCarty 'ired 'im after that. That was afore . . . afore." The liveryman teetered on the edge of saying afore *something*, but stated the second 'afore' as a definite ending. He left the stable and went up the hill east, toward the mansion. Erroll waited with Sampson until the liveryman returned.

"The butler says 'e'll call Pastor MacIntire. Ah'll stay 'ere with Sampson 'till MacIntire gets 'ere."

"I'll stay too. Maybe I should go tell Kenzie."

Kenzie returned to the stable with Erroll. She told the liveryman, "I'll take the horse today and visit the crews. Erroll's in no shape to go, and he wants to stay with Sampson." Erroll saddled a horse and opened the stable door for her. She rode through it and on to the west.

Pastor MacIntire arrived about midmorning. "I talked to a gravedigger. He says he'll dig tomorrow at the Tiny Kirk cemetery, and we can conduct a proper funeral for Sampson tomorrow afternoon."

Erroll looked out the west stable door and asked, "May I dig the grave myself, right beside Poppa's, and may we have the funeral this afternoon, instead of tomorrow afternoon?"

"Is your Poppa dead?"

"Yes, I should have told you at our wedding. He died three days ago."

"I'm so sorry. I didn't know about it, but yes, we can do everything like you want it."

"Thank you, Pastor. Poppa didn't have a proper funeral. Can you do one for him when you finish Sampson's?"

"We can have a joint funeral if you prefer. Will two o'clock work for you?"

"Two o'clock's perfect, but I need to start now." Erroll went back to the shack for the shovel, took it to a spot alongside John's grave, used it to dig, and nearly finished before Kenzie came back about an hour before the funeral. He continued to dig, and didn't accompany Kenzie to the stable.

Kenzie stopped on her way from the stable to the shack and talked to Erroll. "The liveryman told me about the funeral. Will you have the grave ready?"

"Yes, I'm almost done now. You have any trouble putting the horse away?"

"The liveryman did that part."

"Everything satisfactory with the crews?"

"Yes, they said they're so all right I could have stayed away today."

"I'm glad you went. We already missed Monday, and we don't need to miss again."

"I don't know why you care. The boss usually doesn't pay you anyway."

"The boss isn't why I care, but the men need somebody to check on them, and to make sure the boss doesn't do'em dirty. He'd abuse them if he thought he could get away with it, you know."

"I know, and I admire your attitude, but I'm afraid mine doesn't match yours."

Erroll laughed for the first time since he went to the stable hours earlier. "I love you for that, Kenzie. I might hate you if you thought exactly the same as me."

Both Patersons went back to the shack, washed their hands, and changed clothes before Pastor MacIntire arrived. The pastor came with the liveryman, who drove a pair of matched sorrels pulling a flatbed wagon, with Sampson in a new pine box on the wagon.

The pastor spoke only a few words, but included, "I commend your souls to heaven," as he referred to both John and Sampson. Kenzie sobbed when Pastor MacIntire mentioned heaven. Erroll put his arm around her, and then he cried also.

The pastor tried to comfort them. "I didn't know either John or Sampson well. Neither joined Tiny Kirk, but I've spoken with both, and I know as well as I can know about anybody, their souls wait for you in heaven." His words agitated Erroll and Kenzie even more, but he climbed on the wagon seat beside the liveryman and left them to cry beside the two graves.

When they recovered enough to talk, Erroll confessed, "You know, I believe the pastor when he says Poppa and Sampson are in heaven. I don't want to disappoint them if they wait for me and I don't get there."

"Me either. You know how Poppa always read the Bible to us on Sunday? Will you read to me on Sundays too?"

"I'll do it every day from today onward. Another thing I'll do today is carry rocks up here for a monument for Sampson."

Erroll read to Kenzie from the Bible that evening, but she didn't take the privacy curtain down, and he didn't finish the monument for Sampson until the next day.

Chapter 18

1904

A new stable boy greeted Erroll when he checked out a horse on Friday. He claimed to be Dal McCarty, son of Eric. Erroll asked, and Dal further claimed to be fourteen years old. He only needed to get a horse for Erroll, however, and did that without a hitch.

Kenzie removed the privacy curtain while Erroll visited crews on Friday, and moved the table adjacent to the end of the couch, as she called her former bed. John bought a chair when he retired, and she placed it across the table from the couch. She explained, "Now we can both sit down at the table when we eat."

"Looks really great, Kenzie. Where'd your privacy curtain go?"

"Who needs a privacy curtain? We're married, aren't we?"

"Where is it?"

"I used it to make a scarecrow we can use in the garden next summer."

"Great again."

Erroll went back to complete the monument at Sampson's grave after the late noon meal. The boss rode past, going east, before he finished. The boss glared, but didn't slow or stop.

Erroll went to the stable Saturday morning to check out a horse as usual, but Dal ordered, "Stand over there and wait for Mr. McCarty. He wants to speak to you." Erroll stood.

The boss showed up about twenty minutes later. "I visited the crews myself yesterday, and fired the lot of them, effective Monday. You need to get new riffraff on the job by then."

Erroll moved a couple steps closer to his boss. "And why did you fire them?"

"One guy at the far west herd sassed me, and I won't tolerate that."

"I don't plan to sass you. But I do plan to rehire all the men today." Erroll spoke softly.

The boss yelled, "You'll do nothing of the kind, unless you want to end up like Sampson."

Erroll replied softly again. "Sorry, Unc. If you want to ride out Tuesday and check, you'll see the people I'll hire. They'll be the same people you fired yesterday."

The boss's face turned red and his hands trembled. "That's Mister McCarty to you, you scum."

"You're lucky I only called you Uncle, or Unc., or whatever. I could do worse, but that's beside the point. I'm going to rehire the men you fired yesterday." Erroll's quiet tone vanished.

Dal broke in, "Fire' im Paw, he's askin' for it."

"I will Son, but not today. I'll give him all the rope he needs to hang himself."

The boss turned back to Erroll. "Get out of here and don't let me see you again. I might lose control." He stormed out of the stable.

Erroll asked Dal for a horse, and waited until he brought one. He saddled the horse, led him outside, and rode away without further comment. He tried to put out fires when he came to each crew, and discovered how it would go when he talked to Ted at the first herd. "How you doing, Ted?"

"Not good, Erroll. McCarty fired all of us yesterday. I might be able to get another job, but I'm not so sure about Ray and Thomas."

"Don't worry about it, Ted. The boss told me he fired you all, but then he told me to hire more people. That'll be easy—I'll hire you back."

"No, it won't be that easy, Erroll. None of us want to work for McCarty any more."

"I understand, Ted, believe me I do, because I feel the same way.

But I hope you stay, if for no other reason than the cattle need you. You and Ray and Thomas have years of experience among you. You know what the cattle need today, what they'll need tomorrow, and what they'll need come summer. New people would no doubt mean well, but they can't know what you know. As for Ray and Thomas, the best way to help them is to set the example for them, stay, and look out for them the same as always. I need you, too. You're older and more experienced than I am. The only way I can halfway do my job is if you stay. If new people count on me to train them, part of their problem will be I don't know everything they need to know. Will you stay?"

"I don't want to do it, Erroll. I'm sick of McCarty and his superior ways, and I won't even think about it if Ray and Thomas leave."

"How about if I go on to the Middle Valley Herd and the Hummer Bunch, you all talk about it, and tell me what you decided when I come back?"

"That ought 'o work, but don't count on much."

Erroll had a similar conversation at the Middle Valley Herd, but didn't wait until Sunday for the Hummer Bunch decision; he went higher up in the valley to look at the hay supply there. When he came back, Thomas, the new crew leader told him they decided to stay, but, "If McCarty comes back here and fires us again, we'll quit that minute."

"Fair enough, Thomas. I can't predict what the boss might do, but I'll stop him from firing you if I can. I hope you know I will."

"We all know it and we all appreciate it, Erroll, but we don't think you can control the old coot."

"Thanks for whatever you can do. I'll do what I can, and we'll see I guess." Erroll headed back east where each of the other crews agreed to stay, too, but threatened to quit instantly if the boss annoyed them too much. He stopped by the shack to leave the milk and to kiss Kenzie, before he took the horse back to the stable.

Erroll entered the stable, and Dal stated, "You're lucky Paw's not here. He told you to not let him see you."

Erroll answered, "I don't care whether the boss sees me. If I offend him, he can stay away from me, not the other way around. I'm not mad at you, though. If you want me to do anything different when I come in the stable, let me know."

Dal didn't say more, but merely led Erroll's horse away. Erroll went back to the shack and Kenzie asked, "Everything go well today?"

"Not until now. The boss came to the stable and said he fired everybody, so I had to convince them to stay."

"How can you convince them to stay if he fired them?"

"I have authority to hire and fire too, so I merely hired them back, but had to work to persuade them to let me do it."

"What'd you say about the boss mellowing?"

Erroll laughed. "You think I could've been wrong?"

Kenzie laughed, too. "I don't say you could've been, Sir. I say you were."

"You're right when you say I sized him up wrong, but maybe he got it out of his system for a while."

"You want to be wrong again, Erroll?"

"No, but the boss can't be ornery a hundred percent of the time. Can he?"

"Have you seen anything besides ornery?"

"Not yet, but surely he's hiding a good side somewhere. He's my mom's brother after all."

"Neither of us ever knew your mom."

"Yeah, but Poppa did, and he gave a wonderful report. You don't think Poppa lied, do you?"

"I don't think you lie either, but if I die today, you might claim to remember more good things than bad ones."

"Kenzie! Did you marry me under false pretenses? You didn't tell me anything bad about you."

"Right. I'll spring all the bad stuff on you in a big bunch some day."

Erroll grinned. "Anyway, I hope the boss hides all his sides in his mansion, and doesn't cause any more problems for a while."

"You hope for the wonderful, but we both know it isn't realistic."

"We have to wait and see I guess."They joked and laughed and enjoyed all the rest of the day.

Kenzie agreed to go with Erroll on his ride the next day, Sunday, so they walked to the stable, entered, and encountered Dal there. Dal didn't look at Erroll, but stared at Kenzie. "Hi, beautiful lady. Where you been all my life?"

Erroll took a step toward Dal, but Kenzie verbally headed him off. "Mostly being way too old for you, Laddie. Are you big enough to find a horse for us?"

Dal silently walked away and soon returned with a horse. Erroll put a saddle on the horse, and Dal spoke again. "You married to her?"

"Yep."

"Better keep an eye on her. I know when you're gone every day."

"If you lay a hand on her, I'll beat you until you can't walk."

"I ain't gonna lay a hand on her. I'll make her lay hands on me."

"You stay away from Kenzie and from our shack. You understand?"

"You say Kenzie's her name, huh? Kenzie's a purty name. I like it."

Erroll took more steps toward Dal, but Kenzie intervened again. "Nobody cares what you do or don't like. You just do your job here, Laddie, and you won't get into any trouble."

Dal sneered. "I'm family, and you ain't. I can't get in no trouble, but you're already in it."

Kenzie pushed Erroll out the door, where they mounted the horse and went on their way, but Erroll expressed concern. "We have no idea what the kid might do. We gotta think of a way you can get away if he comes to the shack when I'm not there."

"Maybe the best thing is for me to always go with you."

"That'll work most of the time, but you can't always go."

"How about if I put a shell in the rifle and blast him if he gets too close?"

"You'll be in jail the rest of your life."

"Jail might better than to let the little squirt get away with something."

"I almost agree, but there's gotta be a better way."

"Maybe I can pull back some of the steel you installed on the shack for Poppa, and look through a crack to the east every few minutes to watch for him. Perhaps we can borrow a barking dog, or make a little fence around the shack and keep the chickens inside, to sound the alarm."

"I don't like any of it, Kenzie. He can circle around and come from any direction. He can shoot or strangle a dog or chickens. Poppa made a little door out the back for us when we were little, but you can't get through it now. I like your plan to go with me as often as you can, but we need something more. Maybe you can walk over the hill early when you go with me, then I can get the horse and pick you up on the far side of the hill, so he'll never know where you are."

"That sounds like a lot of trouble, and unless I get over there before light, he'll figure it out and can watch. You know that can't work, Erroll."

"Maybe we'll think of something if you go with me for a few days."

"Right. You will even if I don't; you're good at stuff like that."

Kenzie rode with Erroll again on Monday, Tuesday, and Wednesday, and he came back to the Dal problem Wednesday afternoon. "What do you think about riding with me as often as you can, but if the weather's bad or you don't feel like it for any reason, ride with me anyway to the Beauty Firth Beauties shack, and then wait in their shack until I come back? We must clear it with Ted, but I know it'll be all right, and the

Dal kid won't have a chance against three grownups. He might eventually figure it out, but it won't matter except to give him the satisfaction of knowing he got a reaction out of us."

"I can go along with that, but it won't allow me to do anything at our shack. I think I'll end up riding with you almost every time."

"So much the better. If you're all right with it, we'll ask Ted tomorrow." Erroll cleared the plan with Ted, but Kenzie didn't often stay in the other shack, and long before she did, someone trashed the Paterson shack while they visited herds. The person emptied the water bucket on the couch, left the door open so chickens could come in, and tossed a bunch of horse manure around inside.

Erroll and Kenzie cleaned up the shack, and also formed a plan. Erroll checked out a horse the next day as usual. He stopped for Kenzie at the shack as he always did, and they rode over the first hill in their normal way, but then he got off the horse and she went on to visit the crews. He walked up the western side of the hill, out of sight of the mansion, stable, and shack, and circled back east when he came to the trees above the shack. He continued east, and then turned and walked north among the trees on the east side of the stream, until he was even with his shack. Then he stood around and watched. He waited the first day, and nothing happened. When Kenzie returned, he took the horse to the stable as if he'd made his normal run. They repeated the second day, and again nothing happened, so they did it all once more on the third day. Dal left the stable about mid-morning, walked along the road to the path to the shack, and turned up the path toward it. Erroll ran farther down the stream until he came to the road, to cut off a return path to the stable or mansion. Then he ran up the road behind Dal and yelled at him.

Dal turned, and came back to meet Erroll, who asked the obvious question. "Where are you going?"

"To call on Kenzie."

"If I forgot to tell you you're not welcome at our shack, hear me now. I don't ever want to see you at the shack or on this path again."

"I ain't here for you to see me. I'm here for Kenzie to see me."

"I'll step aside and give you three strides start on me. Then I'll chase you all the way to the stable. If I catch you, your paw'll have to get somebody else to run the stable, because you'll never be right again."

Dal almost ran over Erroll. He followed, maintained a separation of about one step, and yelled threats all the way until Dal slammed the stable door shut. Erroll went back to the shack and prepared a late noon meal for Kenzie. When she returned from her work, she asked the usual question. "Anything happen today?"

Erroll informed her something did, but he'd wait to talk about it until he returned the horse. When he led the horse into the stable, Dal took him to a stall as he would on a normal day. Erroll left the stable and went back to the shack.

Kenzie asked, "What happened?"

Erroll told her, and followed up, "We sure can't take a chance on you being here alone if that kid shows up. I may have scared him so bad he won't, but we can never be sure."

Dal played a cat and mouse game with the Patersons for over seven years. Kenzie rode with Erroll almost every day, even though she often wanted to do things at the shack. Dal changed their life from merely difficult to unpleasant, and in return Erroll threatened and insulted Dal repeatedly. The back-and-forth continued until the boss intervened and escalated the unpleasant to intolerable in January of 1912.

Chapter 19

1912

Erroll didn't see his boss for a few years, only Dal. But the boss met Erroll in the stable one morning early in January, a few days before Kenzie and Erroll turned thirty years old. "What do you think of my boy Dal?"

"You might not want to hear."

"He's ready to take on more responsibility. I'm giving him your job today."

"Do you mean I'm fired?"

"That's the size of it. Dal will take over your job, so I won't allow you in the stable, and won't pay you, effective today. You can stay in the shack until August 1. You must be off my estate, and I don't want to see you again after that day."

Erroll didn't visibly react to his firing while he remained in the stable, but shook with anger when he returned to the shack, where Kenzie waited for him to pick her up. He didn't lose a regular wage, because the boss no longer paid regularly, but he did lose the small bonus the boss paid once a year when he sold cattle. He tried to tell Kenzie before she asked, but she spoke first. "Where's the horse?"

"There won't be a horse for us any more. Unc. fired me this morning."

"Wha-at?" Kenzie drew out the vowel sound of the word, and increased the pitch as she neared the end. When Erroll didn't respond quickly she asked, "How will we live?"

"I don't know, Kenzie. I just don't know. The boss said we have to be out of the shack by August 1, so we won't even have a home after that."

"What will happen to the herders?"

"Oh my, Kenzie, I forgot about them. I must go see them all tomorrow and tell them. The boss took the horse away, so I'll have to walk. Dal's bad news for the crews, but potentially bad for you too, and I don't want to leave you alone here. Do you want to go for the entire walk, or do you prefer to stay with the first crew until I get back?"

"I'll walk all the way, so we'll have plenty of time to talk about what we'll do before August."

Kenzie hard-boiled eggs and made pancakes in the afternoon, they awakened before dawn the next day, and went out to walk at first light. They were so early they saw no activity in the first shack. Erroll said, "I didn't expect they'd be up. Let's walk on and we can stop on the way back."

"That'll save some time. I boiled the eggs for lunch, but since we have six and skipped breakfast, do you want one now?"

"Yes, might as well. I'll have one if you will."

"I will."

They walked through the valley, over the ridge to the other side, and could see the Middle Valley Herd before noon. Crew leader George saw them several minutes before they came near enough to talk. He pointed, waved, and everybody in the crew walked toward them. The groups met, and George inquired, "Where's your horse?"

Erroll answered, "Today's not a good day, George. The boss fired me yesterday, but Dal probably already told you that."

George looked intently at Erroll. "Dal?"

"Yes, Dal McCarty. Didn't he tell you he took my place yesterday?"

"No, nobody came yesterday, or today until now; we thought you or Kenzie might be sick or something."

Kenzie said, "We're not physically sick, but we're heartsick about what might happen to each of you. We're afraid the boss won't pay you, or if he does, Dal won't shop for you, or you might have problems we can't predict. The boss up and fired Erroll yesterday, without any warning at all, and Erroll thinks we have to come here to explain, even though we have to walk."

George replied, "I'm glad you did, but you're not gonna walk all the way to the Hummer Bunch today, are you?"

Erroll looked up at the sun. "Yes, so we need to move on."

"Why don't you spend the night in our shack? The sky doesn't look like snow, and we can bed down outside, and leave the whole shack for you."

Erroll shook his head. "We won't hear of it. We expect to be at the Hummer Bunch by noon, and to be back in our shack before dark."

George persisted. "Why don't you turn back now and let one of us walk over to the Hummer Bunch? I can do that."

Kenzie nodded one way, but Erroll the other, so she answered his way. "No, we have plenty of time, and we think we must be the ones to tell them."

"You're probably right. You want a drink of water before you leave here?" Kenzie nodded yes again, Erroll yielded, and they resumed their walk west.

They arrived at the Hummer Bunch shack soon after noon and felt better, because the midday sun took the morning chill off. They told their story, drank almost a liter of water each, turned back east, and ate their pancakes and remaining eggs as they walked. They walked all afternoon, and eventually returned to the Beauty Firth Beauties herd near sundown.

Ted noticed them from a distance and ran to meet them. "Where have you been? We thought something happened to you."

Kenzie responded, "Something did happen to us, and to you, too. I don't suppose Dal told you?"

When Ted shook his head no, Kenzie told him the entire story, and explained they needed to walk on home. Ted insisted he walk to the top of the hill with them, and urged them to come back the next day and every day, to get milk. He added his crew would quit if Dal pestered them, so they'd likely need to arrange with a new crew about milk.

Ted turned back when the group topped the hill, but Erroll and Kenzie continued to walk, and she soon exclaimed, "I see our shack! It never looked good to me before, but it does now. I might be able to walk that far, but perhaps not much farther."

"Same here. As Ted would say, 'I'm fair puggled.' We didn't come up with a decent idea about what we'll do, but why don't we put off further talk about it until tomorrow?"

"I'm for that. I could go to bed as soon as we get there, without any supper except a big long drink of water."

"Me too."

They came to the shack and Erroll commented, "Poppa's watch says we only walked about twenty minutes from the top of the hill. I wonder if the watch is broken? Twenty hours feels more like it to me."

"Yes, twenty or two hundred."

They slept late the next day, because they had no work to do. Erroll questioned Kenzie while she fried eggs and made gravy for breakfast. "How much flour do we have left, and other food?"

"We have most of a twenty kg sack of flour, most of a ham, one small jar of canned apples, and a pile of potatoes under the couch. But we only have about four pounds cash. I think we'll eat a lot of eggs. And you should go get milk today."

Erroll answered, "Neither of us ever had a real job. I don't know who will hire us, or where we can live. We can live in the woods until winter, but then we'll probably die."

"At least for now, Erroll, we live where we can see Beauty Firth, and it's aptly named. We can dip all the water we need out of the stream, and we have a roof over our heads until August 1."

"I'm usually the optimistic one and you're usually more pessimistic. Why the switch?"

"You need to be cheered up, Erroll. We may die in the woods this winter, but you provided everything we need to live until now, and I'll die with no regrets when the time comes."

"That's supposed to cheer me up?"

"All I'm saying is, you've made me happier than any woman in the history of women. And besides, nobody knows when their life will end."

"It's my job to take care of you. So I intend to think about how we can live, not why we must die."

"Of course you're right, Erroll. I'll try to help you be optimistic."

Kenzie and Erroll had no neighbors to support them, no relatives they could count on, no friends able to help them, almost no money, and no influence. Their shack wasn't near other people, no one visited except a bread deliveryman once a week, and Kenzie told him to take them off his list of customers. She asked him to look for a job for Erroll, but nothing came of it. A couple weeks passed, and they tried to have ideas, but nothing came of that effort either.

Kenzie sank deeper into despair despite her promise to be optimistic, and Erroll heard her cry nearly every night. Each of the crews stopped at the shack on separate days in February to say they'd quit, and would look for work in Inverness. Erroll briefly talked about a desperation move. "Kenzie, do you think I should try to get Dal to hire me as a herdsman? I think a new group quits every few days, so he might need somebody."

She screamed at him. "Are you crazy? If Uncle Eric wanted you to work for him, he wouldn't have fired you. Why do you think people quit him after a few days?"

"You're probably right, Kenzie. I won't try for a job with Unc. I know I should try for something, but I don't know what."

They cut back to one meal a day. They sat silently in the shack for hours while Kenzie sketched tombstones and Erroll invented job offers in his mind. They prayed daily for good news, but the only answer they saw was the Tiny Kirk food wagon in mid May.

Chapter 20
1912

Nothing changed until Friday, June 28, barely more than a month before the Patersons' eviction deadline. Someone knocked on the shack door during the early afternoon of that day and Erroll opened the door only a little, as if expecting trouble, and saw someone he'd never seen before.

The stranger identified himself. "I'm Cecil Anderson, US land merchant, selling properties in Texas, Oklahoma, and Missouri."

Kenzie came to stand beside Erroll, and pulled the door open more so she could see the stranger, but spoke tartly. "We've barely heard of those places. We don't have any money. Go away and leave us alone."

Kenzie didn't faze the man, and he went on. "You and your husband are US citizens, right?"

"We are, but we live here now, and we're also UK citizens." Kenzie put her hand on the door.

Erroll invited, "Tell us more."

"I have over thirty properties I can sell, but I'm talking only to US citizens. I have a choice black-land farm in northern Texas, a half-section at only $38 an acre. It has—"

Kenzie broke in. "Mr. Anderson, we don't have any money. We can't buy anything. Nothing. We're broke."

"Well, then, I have just the thing for you. It's in—"

Kenzie interrupted again. "I already told you we don't have any money. It doesn't matter how—"

After Kenzie interrupted, Cecil interrupted in return. "You don't need money. The seller will finance, and will pay your passage to the farm."

Kenzie retorted, "Don't try to fool us with stuff we know can't happen."

She pushed the door, but Erroll caught the edge of it and opened it wide. "Come on in Mr. Anderson. I want to hear more about that seller-financed land." Cecil stepped inside the door and occupied a spot in front of the swinging part.

Kenzie asked, "What exactly must we do in exchange, if he pays our passage?"

"It's not a he, it's a she. Cecelia Shier. Her husband died about four years ago, and left her in a comfortable financial position. She moved—"

Kenzie interrupted yet again. "We don't really need to know about a Mrs. Shier, and we don't need to hear more from you, either."

Everybody fell silent for a moment and Cecil turned toward the door opening, but Erroll persisted. "I want to hear more about that."

Kenzie shrugged and sat on the couch. Cecil turned to face Erroll and continued. "Cecilia doesn't want the burden of the farm, and she moved into town. If you can get to Port Glasgow, she'll pay your steamship fares to New York, plus your train fares to the town of Rounder in west central Missouri, near the land. She'll pick you up in a motorized car, and she'll take you to the house that already stands on the land. I didn't see the land, but she says it's eighty acres, all in grass, and most of it should probably stay that way. She admits the house isn't a palace, but says it has four rooms; it's gotta be a bunch better'n this place." Cecil waved his arm around in a partial circle.

Kenzie re-entered the conversation. "Come on, Mr. Anderson. You know nobody gives stuff away for free. What's the catch? When will we find out what we have to pay for the cost of the trip?"

Cecil replied, "It's in the price of the land."

Kenzie stood up from the couch and opened her mouth, but Erroll spoke first. "When can we actually own the land? And what is that price?"

"It's only $50 an acre. That sounds pretty good to you, right?"

Erroll asked a confirming question. "That would be fifty times eighty or $4,000 total?"

"Yeah, and you'll have a full ten years at no interest. Your payment will only be $400 a year, and the farm should more than make that. So that'll be easy for you, don't you think?"

"What's that in pounds?"

"I think 4,000 US dollars are roughly equivalent to 820 British pounds."

Kenzie objected, "How do we know that's correct?"

Erroll responded, "We know it's at least somewhere near right. Do we need to know more?" Kenzie didn't answer, but merely shrugged and sat on the couch again.

Erroll asked more questions. "And you're sure the travel cost is included? How long will it take to get the money for that? You never did say when we'd own the land."

"I have the actual steamship and railroad tickets instead of money, and can give them to you when you sign this paper. You own the land as soon as you sign." Cecil pulled a partly filled-out sales contract and a pen from his pocket. "May I use your table to fill out details and for you to sign on?"

Kenzie frowned. "What if we don't like it when we see it?"

"What difference will it make? We have nothing here, and whether we like what we find there or not, it'll be more than we have here." Erroll's tone revealed his impatience with the question.

"Maybe you're right, Erroll. But I don't want to buy a pig in a poke and to live out our lives wishing we hadn't."

"Can it be worse to do it than to not do it, and to live out our lives wishing we had?"

"Maybe not. I'll sign if you're sure."

Cecil went to the table, wrote words and numbers on the contract, showed where to sign, and gave the pen to Erroll. Both Patersons signed, and Cecil smiled. "Congratulations, Mr. and Mrs. Paterson. You now own eighty acres of land in Jake County, Missouri." He yanked an envelope from a pants pocket and handed it to Erroll. "Here's your tickets. You might want to look."

Erroll gave the envelope to Kenzie, and she looked. "The tickets seem in order, but how can we know they're are real, this contract is real, and places called Missouri and Rounder really exist?"

Cecil looked out the shack door a moment, and then replied, "It's a real contract, and those places do exist. You have to trust me on that."

Kenzie shrugged again and turned away, but Erroll assured Cecil, "We do trust you, and we thank you for coming here. I lost my job recently, and we need an opportunity like this."

As Cecil moved toward the door opening, he added, "There's one more thing. A US citizen named Tom Schofield lives west of here. Do you know how far west he is?"

Erroll replied, "No, I don't know him, and haven't been as far west as McCarty land goes. Eric McCarty's land goes more than twelve km west."

Cecil went back outside, walked down the path to the road, and turned west. When he reached the road, Erroll hugged and kissed Kenzie. He grinned for the first time in weeks. "How about if we go tomorrow? I think we could take two weeks to walk to Glasgow if we don't push hard."

"Yes, I'm ready for a change of scenery. I hope these so-called tickets get us on some kind of ship when we get there."

"Great. Let's put our stuff in a gunnysack today. We can merely grab it and go, first thing tomorrow."

Kenzie pulled a gunnysack from under the couch, and put their wedding certificate and UK citizenship papers in it, inside a clean jar with a lid. She asked about other items to include. "You think we have enough in the gunnysack Erroll, or should we put more in it?"

"We for sure wanta take Poppa's Bible. Is there a way to keep it dry in case of rain?"

"I can wrap it in oilpaper. I can make a special pocket with a button at the top for your shirt, and you won't have to carry it in the gunnysack."

"That's a good idea—both are good ideas. The oilpaper and the pocket. Can you do the pocket before tomorrow?"

"Yes, it'll look like a patch, but it'll take only a few minutes. What else do we need in the gunny sack?"

"We don't own much, Kenzie. I don't see a reason to carry clothes, and if we don't do that, then food might be the only other thing we need."

"I don't see a need for extra clothes either. We can wash our clothes along with ourselves if we come to a stream, and otherwise we don't need to. So if no clothes, what else besides food, Erroll?"

"What about Poppa's other three books?"

"Do we really need to read recipes? Or accounting or whatever?"

"Probably not, Kenzie, and books are heavy. How much cash did you say we have?"

"We're down to a few pence under two pounds. We for sure must take that, along with the tickets. Maybe it'll be best if we put the money and tickets in the jar too. We can't get to them conveniently, but they'll stay safe and dry there."

"Right. The only other things I can think of then, are matches and food. Can you get matches in the jar?"

"Everything's not in there yet, Erroll, but I'm sure I can crowd them in. Should I put Poppa's watch in there as well, or will it be enough to wrap it in oil paper?"

"How about the watch in the jar? And as for food, we'll probably want more than we can take."

Kenzie nodded. "Probably. I already know we have five eggs. Our young chickens are still a little under-sized, but I'll fry two this evening.

We don't have potatoes under the couch, and those in the garden are small, but we can dig as many as you want to carry. I'm not sure how we can cook them. Maybe you can cut sticks with Poppa's pocketknife and we can hold them over a fire."

"Yeah, maybe. I'll take the gunnysack up to the garden when you finish with it, and dig as many potatoes as I wanta carry. I can't catch chickens until they roost this evening, but maybe that'll be soon enough."

"Yes, it'll be fine."

Erroll went to the garden and dug several potato hills. He estimated it would take two weeks to walk to Glasgow, so he selected the twenty-eight biggest potatoes he found, and put them in the gunnysack. He came back and built a fire in front of the shack, so Kenzie could hard-boil the eggs and fry the chickens he intended to catch.

They didn't quickly fall asleep that night, but talked instead. Erroll overflowed with optimism. "I know cattle. We'll get some to put on our farm and we'll have milk and beef to sell every year. Our contract calls for only $400 payments and those'll be easy. We'll be the McCartys of Missouri."

Kenzie questioned Erroll's predictions. "You expect a lot, even if the farm's not a hoax, and if we can travel to it. People won't give cattle to us. Can we find them for sale, can we pay for them, and can we sell anything the first year? Can we cope with winter there? Will we need more feed than just grass, and if we do, can we pay for it? Can we survive until the farm makes a profit?"

Erroll frowned in the darkness. "How can we know about such details? We have to wait and see . . . We can't be any worse off in Missouri than we are here."

"You're right about that last. I hope all the other works out."

Erroll put his arm over Kenzie, comforted her, and offered, "We can't know, but it won't help to worry about it."

They slept for only short periods that night, and suffered longer episodes of wakefulness. Erroll got up twice to check for signs of sun, but found none either time. He got up a third time. "I'm gonna look out the door and see if I see any light in the east."

"Don't bother. Let's get up and start. We don't need light until we turn south from Inverness, anyway."

"I'll look, just in case." He went to the door and spoke to already upright Kenzie. "I think I see a trace of light. Are we all ready to go?"

"Not completely. Don't you think you should put your pants and shoes on?"

"Oh, yeah. I can do that quick. Except for clothes, are we ready?"

"I need shoes, too, but then I think we're ready. The gunnysack's right there by the fireplace."

They couldn't take a last look at the inside of the shack, because they didn't have a light inside. They took a last look at their latrines outside, however, carefully closed the shack door for the last time, and headed down the path to the road for the last time. Kenzie commented, "We should try to squeeze out a tear, because we'll never see our childhood home again."

Erroll jumped over a puddle in the road and grinned. "Cry all you want. I don't wanta see that miserable shack again anyway." He sobered when he judged they might be about even with John's and Sampson's graves, removed his hat, and carried it in his hand until they crossed the bridge at the lower edge of the Big Wood.

Kenzie didn't respond to Erroll until they crossed the stream. Then she said, "I never want to be shut in that hut either, or to see Dumb Dal again, and if we make it past the mansion one more time, he'll never know where we went."

Erroll's shoulders tensed. "Oh, I nearly forgot about Dal. I wish we could go another way, but the odds are he won't come out before we pass by, because it's pretty early." However, they walked a mere ten more meters before they saw light flood out an open door at the

McCarty mansion. "Oops. That's probably him. We're gonna have to see him one more time."

"Quick, Erroll. Why don't we hide beside the road until he goes into the stable?"

"If he knew we did that, it'd make him happy. I'm not afraid of him. I don't want to see him, but I can handle him and he knows it."

"Yes, but why ask for trouble?"

"Too late. I think he sees us. Lets walk on as if we don't see him."

Dal approached and held up his lantern. "You guys are out pretty early aren't you? You afraid to let Kenzie out alone in the dark, Erroll?"

Kenzie answered instantly. "You hush up Laddie. Go on to the stable and do your job."

Dal came closer. "I ain't Laddie no more, or didn't you notice? I'm full-growed now."

Kenzie retorted, "You may be 'full-growed' physically, but your mind is that of a twelve-year-old."

Erroll interjected, "We're out for a walk and don't want trouble. We're headed for Glasgow and we'll walk on."

Dal didn't give up. "That's right. You walk one way, and me and Kenzie's gonna walk the other way." Dal put his hand on Kenzie's shoulder and pushed her backward so hard she stumbled. "Mach a Seo!"

Erroll temporarily lost his mind. He knocked Dal down with one punch to the chest and bellowed, "Get up out of the mud, Dal, and don't mess with grown-ups. You go on down to the stable and do your job, like Kenzie said. I'll stand here until I see you go in. If you stop anywhere I'll come back down the hill and break every bone in your body."

Dal threatened, "My paw ain't gonna like this a wee bit. You better watch your step, mister tough guy."

Chapter 21

1912

Erroll didn't react, but when Dal struggled to his feet, he stood and watched Dal into the stable, as he promised. He told Kenzie, "I think that's our last meet-up with Dal, and it can't come too soon. I'll probably kill'im if a next time happens."

Kenzie laughed. "Erroll! I thought you said you intended to be a Christian like Poppa!"

Erroll frowned. "I don't see anything funny about it. Dal acts like a man who wants his face smashed; I ache to make his wish come true, and I might do it if I see him again."

Kenzie replied more soberly, "Calm down, Erroll. I hope we won't. Ever see him again, that is. Let's walk; we have more light now."

They walked in silence for a while, and then Kenzie asked, "Do you remember what the Port in Glasgow looks like?"

"I can only see a few scenes from it in my mind's eye. Why?"

"I don't remember much either. I wonder if we should stay out of sight there?"

"Why, Kenzie?"

"Old Eric's a powerful guy in Scotland. Do you suppose he'll send people to stop us from getting on the ship?"

"You're silly."

"Perhaps. Do you know where the road south out of Inverness is?"

"No, but there's probably only one, and it shouldn't be hard to find." The sun appeared on the eastern horizon just before Erroll and Kenzie came to Inverness. The light revealed slightly emaciated, but fit thirty-year-olds. Erroll stood a good 180 cm tall, sported sandy hair, freckles, and a weathered face. The shorter Kenzie's long black hair framed her face and neck; she moved with an easy stride, as did Erroll.

Erroll suggested, "Let's take each south street we come to, and turn east when we can't go south. We'll sooner or later come to a road south out of Inverness, and on to Glasgow."

Kenzie accepted the plan, but they soon encountered confusing and unfamiliar streets. Their confidence faded, and Kenzie suggested they spend some of their money to buy a map. Erroll agreed, so they entered a store, and bought a map of Scotland. They came out of the store and looked at the map. Kenzie exclaimed, "Wow! We better hang on to this map. The roads look pretty tangled."

"Yeah. Let's study this thing and plan a route." They located Inverness and Glasgow on the map soon, but required more time to see a clear path between the two. Erroll eventually traced a path with his finger. "This Great Glen Way looks best, past all these lochs to Ballachulish. The same road turns east there before it heads south again to Glasgow. The road crooks and turns a lot, but might be the best we can do. And maybe we won't get lost if we stay on that one road."

They retraced part of their recent route, asked a few passersby, found the road they wanted, and turned south. Kenzie inquired, "How far must we walk each day?"

"We don't need to kill ourselves. I don't know how often a ship leaves Glasgow for the US, but if we get there too late for one, there'll surely be another in a few days. It's about 210 km to Glasgow from here, so if we average . . . fifteen km a day, we should get there in two weeks. We only need to walk five km per hour for three hours to do our fifteen, so let's be sure we walk three hours each day and then do any more we feel up to."

"Wonderful. Let's walk six or seven hours today, to get a good start."

"All right, but a thing to watch out for is to walk too long, and then be too tired to build our fire, and too lazy to walk three hours the next day."

They walked two more hours and came to a bridge over the Caledonian Canal. They saw an obvious camping spot barely north of the bridge, adorned with ashes from someone's earlier campfire. They stopped and scrambled down from the road to the campsite. Erroll set the gunnysack on the ground, pulled out the jar, then John's pocket watch, and reported, "It's only 10:30. This travel business is easier than working for the boss."

"Ha. Let's wait a couple weeks, and see if we still think that."

Erroll grinned and shook his head at Kenzie's outlook. "What can go wrong? We have a map and a road all the way. We completed our first day and we're not tired."

"Yes, Erroll, I feel a little lazy to stop now, but this campsite is so perfect. We might like it better here than we did in our shack. We'll feel cooler, and maybe we don't even need a fire. You want lunch early? We skipped breakfast this morning, and I'm hungry. I'll dig around in the gunnysack and find a fried chicken to put with an egg apiece, and those should hold us fine until evening. Maybe a fire and a potato then?"

"That all sounds great to me. We might even save a couple chicken wings and forget the potato."

"We can skip the potato, but you said we have twenty-eight, and I wonder how they taste roasted on a stick."

A carriage traveled across the bridge above them before they ate their noon meal. Erroll glanced casually at the carriage, pulled by two high-stepping matched sorrels, and then stared intently at the horses. "Did you recognize those horses when they went by?"

"Yes, they're McCarty's. I told you he'd send somebody to look for us."

"You know what? We need to forget the fire tonight, and tomorrow we must stay off the road and walk far enough to the side nobody can see us from it."

Kenzie frowned. "I think you're right. Our walk will be tougher, though."

"Yes, a lot tougher. I think we're all right here for tonight if we don't start a fire." But after a moment, Erroll said, "On the other hand, it won't hurt to move downstream to put a few more trees between us and the road. Let's do it quick, before somebody else comes down the road. Do you remember if I told Dal where we intend to go?"

"I sure do. You told him we're walking to Glasgow."

"Oh, no. Why did I do that? I never dreamed he'd try to find us. I suppose he'll just wait for us at a bridge or a mountain pass."

"Perhaps we ought to change our route to something less direct. Maybe Dal won't figure it out."

Erroll frowned. "Yes, but maybe he will. We'll never understand how Dal thinks."

"That's if he thinks. But I suppose you're right." They walked about thirty meters down the canal and then closer to it behind a grove of trees. They ate a fried chicken and saved some, plus they saved the eggs they intended to eat. They smoothed off a spot to lollygag on, and to sleep on later, and then emptied their pockets and took a dip in the canal to wash their clothes and themselves. Their clothes stayed wet most of the day, but it was almost July, and they said the wet clothes felt good. They laughed and joked for most of the afternoon.

They slept well that night, and awakened barely before sunup. They lacked ambition when they first waked up, skipped breakfast, and talked a few minutes. Erroll proposed, "I think we should try to keep the road in sight as much as possible, so we don't get lost, but we need to stay far enough away from it that people on it won't notice us."

"Whatever you say, Erroll. You think we should look at the map?"

"Yeah, probably." Erroll removed the map from the jar in the gunnysack, they studied it, and then he resumed. "We should go back to the road, wait until nobody's in sight, and then run across the

Caledonian Canal bridge, and across the road to the east side, because I'm sure we can walk beside the canal easier than beside the road. We can stay close to the canal until it comes back to the road by Loch Dochfour, then we'll have to cross the road again and walk west of it, west of the loch, and west of Loch Ness. Maybe we can make it to Drumnadrochit today. That might be sixteen or seventeen km, but I think it's a reasonable target."

"Whatever you think, Erroll. Do you think we can go all the way before we stop to eat?"

"We'll be hungry, but it makes sense to me."

"Let's do it."

"If you're willing to do it, Kenzie, I am too."

They walked back upstream alongside the canal until they came close to the road, approached it cautiously, chose a time to run across the canal bridge and across the road, and made it safely. The road and the canal diverged. They stayed close to the canal and walked steadily through tall grass and an occasional wood, but were ready to stop and rest when the road and canal came back together, north of Loch Dochfour. Trees covered the convergence point, so they walked within twenty meters of the road before they stopped to look at the map again.

Erroll worried, "Do you think you can go on, Kenzie?"

"Yes, but a little rest'll feel good."

"Same here. When we start again, we need to sneak up to the road, wait for a good time, and run across to the west side. Then we can get as far away from the road as we think we need to, and turn south again, to keep the road in sight."

After Kenzie rested, they crossed the road according to Erroll's plan, and found a tree-covered strip close to it, with open pasture a little farther west. Erroll changed the plan. "Maybe it's better to stay close to these trees and if we hear a horse or a carriage, we can hide behind the trees. That's probably better than if we're over there,"

Erroll pointed west, "more in the open." They followed the new plan, but soon came to the north shore of Loch Dochfour.

Kenzie asked, "Does the map show this loch right here?"

Erroll retrieved the map from the gunnysack to look. "Yes. It shows our road on a built-up strip cutting across the corner of the loch. If we stay to the north and west of the loch, the map says the road will eventually come back to the west edge of it."

"How far do we have to walk before that happens?"

Erroll looked at the map again. "Maybe a km to a km and a half."

"How far from Drumnadrochit are we?"

"Maybe ten to twelve km."

"What time is it?"

Erroll looked at John's pocket watch. "It's 9:38."

"How long do you think it will take to walk to Drumnadrochit?"

"Unless we pick up speed, we could take until 12:30 maybe, or a little longer."

"Wow, Erroll, I'm tired already. Do you think it will make sense if we only walk until about eleven o'clock and stop?"

"I want to get there, Kenzie, and we're only on our second day. But I don't want to wear you out today so you can't walk much tomorrow. We can stop whenever you think it's time."

"I could stop now. How about if we do that, eat the other three eggs and only part of the fried chicken, rest an hour, and then walk on for only a couple more hours?"

"We can do that, or we can call it a day here if you want to."

They stopped, and then resumed at eleven o'clock. Kenzie said she found a second wind, but Erroll insisted they stop at one o'clock, three to five km short of Drumnadrochit. They rested, built a fire, roasted four potatoes, and ate the remaining chicken. They went to sleep early, awakened early, and started to walk early.

Erroll walked slower the third day, and Kenzie didn't complain about being tired. The map showed Drumnadrochit over a mile west of Loch Ness, and their road veered over to it. They walked west of the road, but when it turned west toward the city, Erroll suggested, "Why don't we cross the road here and cut off three km of walking?"

"Anything to cut off three km sounds great to me." They crossed, and instead of walking roughly four km, walked only about one, but it was a tough one km. They struggled through a wooded area, and had to find places to wade two streams. Their gunnysack no longer contained food other than raw potatoes, but Erroll scared up a young rabbit while in the woods, ran it down, and caught it. He built a fire and they sat while Kenzie cooked it. They eventually walked more, and crossed their road again.

After they crossed safely and walked away from the road east of Drumnadrochit, Kenzie bragged, "I feel great today. I don't know why I felt so tired yesterday, but I can go on and on today. What's our target today?"

"We don't have a target. Let's get the map out and choose one."

Kenzie looked over Erroll's shoulder and chose a target. "How about Invermoriston? How far is that from here?"

"It looks like only six to eight km. That might be all we want today, but if we get there and feel great, we can set another target. How's that?"

"Sounds good, Erroll."

They resumed their walk and stayed close to their road and west of it, but discovered rough terrain. Then they came to the Creag-nan-Eun Forest, even worse to walk through, but by noon they could see Invermoriston. Erroll asked, "Do you feel like walking around it, so we can start tomorrow on the other side? Maybe it's small."

"I'm pretty shot, but I think I can hold out that long. Let's do it."

They began to walk around, with Erroll in front, but he stopped. "Hear that Kenzie?"

"What is it?"

"I think it's a waterfall. If there's a river here, it could stop us."

A voice came from behind Kenzie. "Yeah, it'll stop ye all right. Who are ye?"

Chapter 22

1912

The Patersons whirled around to look back. Erroll couldn't speak for a moment, but when he could, he answered, "We're from up north. Who are you?"

"Ah'm Ed McDowell, the grocer in Invermoriston. What'd ye say your names are?"

"I'm Erroll Paterson and this is my wife, Kenzie."

"What're ye doin' off out 'ere in th' woods?"

"It's a long story."

"Tell me."

Erroll described their plans, explained why, and why they didn't want to travel on the road. Ed said he understood. "Yeah, Ah've 'eard about th' McCartys. A sorry lot they be. Ye must be tired."

Kenzie nodded. "You can say that again. But the McCartys are our main problem. You won't tell anybody about us will you?"

"Never. Will ye stay the night with ma wife and me? Ah can take ye across th' bridge on ma oxcart tomorrow if ye will. No McCarty'd think t' look twice at three people on a' oxcart."

Kenzie clutched Erroll's arm and smiled. "Oh Mr. McDowell, will you? That will help us so much."

They went with Ed to his home, where he and Mrs. McDowell provided a couch to sleep on, along with food, bath water, and temporary clothes to wear while they washed their other clothes. They pushed to go when morning came, but Ed observed, "Looks like it could rain t'day, and when it looks rainy 'ere in Invermoriston, it us'lly rains . . . maybe ye ought t' stay 'ere another day."

Both in response to Ed, and to Erroll's frown, Kenzie said, "We do appreciate what you did for us—everything—but we want to get to Glasgow as soon as we can. We really must go; rain won't hinder us."

Ed countered, "Ye ain't dressed for rain. Rain's cold 'ere, and with those summer clothes ye 'ave, ye'll be cold awhile at best. And if it rains, ye'll think ye're about t' freeze t' death."

Erroll asserted, "We'll go."

"Whateffer. If ye're dead set on goin', I'll find a couple loaves o' day old bread from th' store around 'ere, and a chunk o' cheese ye can take. Ye gotta eat."

Kenzie replied, "Thank you Mr. McDowell. We started with not much, and even that's mostly gone."

Ed gave them the food and took them across the bridge as he promised. They didn't see McCarty people, but a cold misty rain began as they approached the bridge.

Ed tried again before the Patersons jumped down off the oxcart. "Its turrible snell, 'specially with that smirr—"

Kenzie interjected, "What?"

"Th' air's cold, and th' rain makes it worse. Ye sure ye won't come back with me, and wait 'till tomorrow?"

Erroll shook his head. "No, we already decided. Like Kenzie said, we're grateful to you, more than you can know, but we'll get off here. This is the road to Glasgow?"

Ed pointed south, and replied, "This 'ere's it."

They hopped off the oxcart on the right side and left the road on that same side—the west side. The road soon turned mostly east to follow River Moriston. Trees shielded them from the road for three hundred meters or so along it, enough for the road to curve back toward the south, but they came to a grassy area. They could see trees beyond, but stopped before entering the open space between. Kenzie suggested, "Maybe we ought to look at the map."

Erroll resisted. "I hate to get it out in the rain. Maybe we can find a dryer place somewhere."

"The wind seems to be out of the north. I can face north and you can hold the map against my back."

"We don't need to do it. We looked at it back at the McDowell's so we know what we'll see. The road hugs the west shore of Loch Ness all the way to Fort Augustus, and that'll be about eleven km."

"You're probably right, Erroll, but I don't want to walk all day beside a wrong road, especially in this rain. I'm about to shiver my teeth out."

"This isn't a wrong road. I know what we'll see if we look at the map because we already looked." He looked at the sky. "I'm cold too, and I don't see any breaks in the clouds. What are we gonna do about this open place?"

"I'm so miserable I don't much care. Can we gamble and walk straight through it?"

"I don't like to take the risk, but we might get away with it. I'm game if you are. Let's head for those trees."

The open space extended about five hundred meters, but they made it across. Rain intensified to a hard shower before they reached the trees, but after a few minutes went back to the same fine mist as before. Trees lined the road south to Fort Augustus, but concealed steep and muddy terrain. Because the land sloped up sharply, with no level space between the road and the ridge beside it, they both tired quickly. Kenzie noted, "The ridge above us looks like it goes on and on. Should we go up to the top and hope for more level walking up there?"

Erroll wiped water off his face. "We can try it. The wind might be stronger up there, but maybe there'll be fewer trees, and we'll get more sun if it ever comes out."

They went up the slope and found better walking conditions, with exceptions where they had to pick their way down into glens then back out, but the rain continued with only short breaks. Erroll mentioned another problem when they saw Fort Augustus ahead. "The map showed River Oich at Fort Augustus, plus something else, maybe a canal. The map showed them both to be wide. I think we have to return to the road and go across on bridges, but we'll take a chance if we do it."

Kenzie grimaced. "If Dal intends to wait for us, he probably plans to do it at a place he knows we have to go, like a bridge. I don't know if we should try it."

"We can go down there and look, but short of a miracle, it seems likely there's no other way." The rain strengthened as he spoke.

"We can't stop. Maybe you're right."

Erroll tried to make the risk sound better to Kenzie. "How about if we try to invent a disguise?"

"Like what?"

"Maybe we can separate. You can pull your bonnet down over your face and go on ahead. I'll come along close enough behind to always be able to see you. That's not much of a disguise, but Dal may expect us to be together, and if he sees one person, maybe he won't notice. He's not overly smart, you know."

"That should at least help, Erroll. Perhaps we can look around for a walking stick for me to carry and I can walk bent over like an old woman. Maybe that'll fool him. But what about you? If he recognizes you, he'll know I'm nearby, or if he catches me, it won't take him long to see you too."

"I can pull my hat down too. Maybe we can stuff some leaves under my shirt to change my shape, and I can walk like an old person as well. I think the map showed two bridges, and they're the only way across. We can start now to look for a stick, but let's wait until we're closer to the road to put leaves in my shirt."

"Erroll, you're so smart! I don't know if it'll work, but a disguise sounds like the best and only plan better than to merely hope Dal won't be there."

They found a stick and eventually approached the road. Erroll cautiously looked up the road and down it. "Kenzie, those sorrels are down there by the bridge. You think we ought to wait until they leave?"

"No, I want to go now. We're cold and wet, and we can't start a fire because the wood's wet too. The bread Ed gave us is probably soggy. Why don't we each have just one bite of cheese and pass by those horses like we don't know them. Maybe then we can walk until the rain stops. I sure hope it'll stop sometime today."

Kenzie stuffed leaves under Erroll's shirt. "Wow, Kenzie! Those are cold. Can't you find dry ones?"

"Sorry, Erroll, wet's all we have today."

"The front of the McCarty coach is on this end. Don't look when you go past it. You might be in the clear when you get by, but even so, walk on a ways before you get off the road so as to not be too obvious. Get off the road on the right."

"Yes Erroll, you be careful too. How dumb do you think I am? Here I go."

They walked past the carriage, and across both bridges without incident, and came together again about two hundred meters behind the carriage, behind three trees west of the road.

"Did you see who was in the carriage Erroll?"

"No, we said we wouldn't look, remember?"

"I didn't, but I saw Dal out of the corner of my eye. He didn't look at me."

"Really? Maybe he doesn't expect us to come through here on a rainy day. Maybe when he doesn't see us, he'll give up and go back to his mansion."

"Do you really think that, Erroll?"

"Do you really think Dal will spend days on end chasing you, Kenzie?"

"We have to allow for that possibility, don't we?"

"Yes, I suppose so." Erroll looked at the sky. "I see a little light in the west, so maybe this stupid rain will stop before night. If it does or doesn't, I think we should walk a little farther, because I saw one of the horses we used to ride tied to a bridge rail behind the McCarty carriage. I didn't see anybody around, but the horse recognized me, and I think there's more than just Dal around here."

"Yes, I saw the horse too. I didn't plan to tell you."

"Kenzie! We have to see everything we can, and tell each other what we see."

"Well, I know you're right. The horse is all I saw, and I agree we should go on, but unless you know what the map shows past Fort Augustus, we need to look at it."

"Yes, but I still don't want to get it out in the rain."

"So maybe we'd better stop."

"Probably, but not right here. Let's go at least a little farther." They turned to go, but Erroll pushed Kenzie down and crouched beside her. "Shh!" A man walked up the road toward the McCarty carriage. They watched him until he was nearly out of earshot, then Erroll whispered, "Do you know who that is?"

Kenzie whispered back, "No."

"He's the boss's butler. I wonder how many more McCarty people are around here?"

"I don't know, Erroll. This place is plumb creepy. Let's go." They walked along the west side of the road for only about five minutes.

Erroll looked at the sky again and fretted, "I don't like this. We ought to get farther from the road, but the river's right over there." Erroll pointed west. "Maybe we're on the wrong side of the road. Let's stop behind these trees." Erroll pointed to some trees up ahead. "I wish the rain'd stop. I'm like you, I don't want to go too far until we look at the map. You hungry?" They walked to the tree cover Erroll selected.

Kenzie didn't respond to Erroll's question until they reached the trees. Then, "You asked if I'm hungry. I could eat dirt! How about you?"

"I'm close to the dirt stage, maybe not quite there. You think it's safe to eat here?"

"Probably no different than to merely stand here."

Erroll set the gunnysack on the ground and looked inside. "Wow. I don't think we can get the bread out. Most of it's scattered, and stuck all over the potatoes."

"That's terrible. We should have eaten it first thing. What about the cheese?"

"The cheese looks fine. Let's split it."

"Let's do. How much is there?"

Erroll looked again. "There's a lot, but maybe not as much as we want."

"Get it."

Erroll pulled the cheese out of the gunnysack, wiped clinging bread off it, and broke it into two pieces, one slightly larger than the other. He offered the bigger piece to Kenzie.

"Are you sure you don't want the big one?"

"Yes, take it." Kenzie took it. They devoured the cheese and could have eaten more. The rain slowed while they ate, and although it didn't entirely stop, Erroll got the map out of the gunnysack. They looked at it hurriedly, Erroll put it back in the jar, and returned the jar to the gunnysack.

"Maybe we should stay on this side of the road. It looks like the next obstacle is Loch Uanagan and the road goes along the east side of it. But the loch's only about eight hundred meters long, so we can go around it on the west side and we'll be back by the road when we get around the loch. Does that sound like it'll work?"

"I'm with you, Erroll. If you think it will, then I agree."

"We probably can't make it to Loch Uanagan today, because it's too far. What if we walk for an hour, and then if the rain stops, look for a place well off the road where we can build a fire and stack up some leaves or something to get a dry place to sleep?"

"I can hold out that long if you can."

They walked about five km beyond Fort Augustus. The rain ended, so when they saw scrubby trees on a slope to their west, they walked toward them across an open space, and continued up the slope until they went through a dense brushy strip. Erroll commented, "Those trees behind us should hide a fire, so what we need to do now is find a place we can make dry, and find water to drink. I can drink liters." Erroll set the gunnysack on the ground and looked first for a stream. He found a small one with a little pool in it about twenty meters to the north, and had a big drink.

He came back to Kenzie. "I found water. I'll show you." He did, Kenzie had a big drink, then Erroll had another, and Kenzie followed with another.

Kenzie apologized, "I tried to make a place to sleep. It'll be lumpy, but I don't know how to do better. All I did was place some dead limbs against each other to keep us off the wet ground. Maybe we can eventually use leaves to cushion us from the limbs, but the leaves are all soaking wet now."

"That's probably the best we can do Kenzie. As tired as we are, we'll probably never notice."

"What time is it?"

Erroll got John's pocket watch out of the jar, looked at it, and replied, "It's 1:30. We either covered a lot of km today or we walked slow, probably the latter. I'm ready to try out that bed right now, without leaves. A fire'd feel great, but we can't build one until the wood dries, and I'm too tired to wait."

Kenzie answered, "I think I'll lie down too." They did, and went quickly to sleep. They remained asleep until a voice from atop a horse awakened them.

Chapter 23.

1912

The voice startled them, but when they saw the boss's liveryman stare down at them from the back of the horse they saw by the bridge, they felt terror. Erroll struggled to stand, but words flowed out before he did. "If that Dal so much as touches Kenzie—"

The liveryman interrupted. "Ye're great people like your paw before ye. Dal's no good, and 'is paw ain't neither, so Ah ain't gonna tell on ye. Ah seen ye come up 'ere, and figgered who ye are. Ah wanted t' make sure, but Ah'll see nobody else comes up 'ere."

Words then poured from Kenzie. "How can we know you won't tell? How can we know you won't bring a great horde of McCartys up here in a few minutes?"

"Ye can believe me or not, but Ah won't. Your best bet is t' stay right 'ere. Ah'll try t' get Dal t' go somewhere away from that bridge afore dark, and if 'e wants t' come up 'ere, Ah'll tell'im Ah a'ready been 'ere and seen nary trace of ye."

Erroll asked, "How many of them are after us?"

"Only three. Me and Dal and th' butler. Me nor th' butler'll breathe a peep if we see ye, but we won't go up 'gainst Dal if 'e sees ye. Ah'm gonna go up on th' ridge top and make a show o' lookin' for ye."

Erroll asked another question. "Wait! What does Dal expect to do if he catches us?"

"'E's gonna 'ave the polis take ye back t' Inverness t' face a' assault charge." After a pause, "'E 'as 'is paw's rifle. Ah think 'e 'opes ye'll give'im a reason t' shoot ye." After another pause, "It's time t' go."

The liveryman rode to the top of the hill and Erroll looked at Kenzie. "You think he's telling the truth?"

"We have to believe him don't we? If he's not telling the truth, the jig is up for us, whatever we do. I don't like the sound of that rifle talk."

"Me either. I wanted to stand close to a fire and get dry tonight, but now I don't think we should build one, because somebody might see it. Maybe we can move the tree limbs over by the water or somewhere, and then take turns staying awake."

"For what, Erroll? If somebody comes up here, we can't get away, and if we know a couple minutes sooner, how will it help?"

"If somebody comes up here to murder me, I prefer to be awake for it."

Kenzie shrugged. "Stay awake if you want to. I intend to sleep tonight."

"What about moving the tree limbs?"

"I agree about not building a fire, but about nothing else."

They tried again to sleep when night came, didn't move the tree limbs, slept fitfully, and the liveryman kept his word. They arose, still shivering. Their clothes remained wet all night, but they didn't drip water in the morning, as they did the day before. They looked at the map and Erroll made a plan for the day. "We can continue south like we said yesterday, and go around Loch Uanagan like we said. We need to be careful not only for ourselves, but for the liveryman as well, because if Dal finds out he lied to him, the liveryman will be in trouble." Erroll looked at the map more. "We're only six or seven km from Invergarry, and there's another bridge to cross after we pass there. Maybe we should find a place to camp before we cross the bridge, go back into town, and leave some false clues."

"False clues?"

"Yes, we can identify ourselves and say we're looking for a boat to take us through Loch Ness to Inverness. We can talk to as many people as possible about that."

"Won't that be dishonest, Erroll?"

"You think it's wrong, in light of the threat we face?"

"I'm not sure. But if we tell people who we are, that'll give Dal a fix on our progress. And after you told him we're walking to Glasgow, will he believe we walked all this way just to go back? Do we want to lie as part of a tactic that probably won't work anyway?"

Erroll waved his hand dismissively. "We can't be picky about right or wrong, and Dal's dumber than we can probably imagine."

"You're right about Dal being dumb. I don't know if false clues are wrong, but I do know you're wrong when you say we can't be picky. Dal's not picky about right or wrong, and that's why he's Dal. If we don't want to be like him, then we need to care about what's right and what's wrong."

"You probably make sense, Kenzie. But if we don't plant false clues, then we don't have a strategy to make Dal lose track of us. Since we don't, how about if we go almost to the bridge today, I sneak up and look, and if I see anything McCarty, we wait another day, and if need be more days, until Dal gives up?"

"That's a better plan, Erroll. How far is it to the next bridge?"

"Maybe seven km, eight or ten at the most."

"That might be a terribly long distance, depending on how rough it turns out to be, but perhaps we can find a better place to camp when we get there. We might as well wait to eat until then, because we don't have anything except potatoes."

They walked. They found a wild plum tree and ate plums until their stomachs hurt. Their route went through difficult terrain again, and they didn't make good time, but before noon they came a curve where the road turns west to Invergarry. They looked for a place to camp, found a spot well hidden by trees, near water, and smooth enough to sleep on. They rested a few minutes, and then Erroll said, "I'm gonna go beside the road to the bridge and look for McCarty horses." He came back after a while and reported, "I didn't see anything, but we've gone far enough today. We can cross tomorrow if I don't see anything then, but even if I don't, we probably should do our disguise thing again."

"I know I should argue with you about stopping, but I'm worn out and am ready to stop. You think we can risk a fire now?"

"Yes, better now than after dark. I spent the early part of the morning wanting to dry my clothes, but now I'm hot and wish they were wet again."

Erroll built the fire, they roasted potatoes, and put the fire out. They slept soundly all night and didn't awaken until bright sunlight came through the trees.

Kenzie woke first, and waited for Erroll. When he awoke she asked, "What do you think are the chances Dal's waiting at the bridge?"

Erroll frowned. "How can I know, Kenzie? We have to look."

"Do you think we should put on our disguises here, both go, and move right on across if the coast is clear?"

"Yeah, that'll save time if nobody's there."

"Should we look at the map here, before we start?"

"Probably as good a time as any. I'll find it." As Erroll looked for the jar in the gunnysack he observed, "There's bread stuff all over everything in this gunnysack. I suppose it'll dry and maybe won't hurt anything." He unfolded the map and touched it with his finger. "Here's where we are." He moved his finger and continued, "There's the bridge where we want to go. There's another bridge not much farther." He folded the map. "I think we want to walk down the west side of the road after we cross the first bridge today, and then switch to the east side if we cross the second. The trip to Spean Bridge along the edge of Loch Lochy will be a long thirty km if we cross both bridges today. Maybe we should make two days out of that distance."

"I agree, Erroll. That many km wouldn't have sounded bad before we left, but even half of that sounds tough to me now. I'm for making two days out of it, or perhaps even three."

"Good. We can plan two, but change later if we think we must. We won't know when we're halfway, but maybe we can guess."

They donned their disguises, and Erroll carefully approached the road near the bridge. He saw nobody, and beckoned for Kenzie. They walked separately across the bridge and met off the road to the west as before.

Kenzie inquired, "Should we keep our disguises?"

"Your disguise isn't anything except a walking stick, so you might as well hang on to it. Mine's only leaves, but they're itchy, so I think I'll get rid of them and get more when we need them."

They traveled roughly five km to the second bridge and walked across that too, then walked more, east of the road. Thick woods covered the land beside the road, and a steep slope made it hard for them to walk. They nevertheless continued, took a good long rest when they went through one of the several patches of wild dewberries they saw, and walked again. A young rabbit jumped up in front of them, but Erroll didn't chase it. They stopped by water around noon, and abundant trees hid them from the road.

Kenzie plopped down, sighed, and asked, "Do you think we'll make it?"

"What a question, Kenzie! Of course we'll make it. We planned to make it from the start."

"Well, we've walked and walked, and we're not even half way."

"Do you think we walk too fast?"

She sighed again. "That and more. Sometimes we see houses in the distance and I imagine women in them, women with children, food and water, good beds, bathtubs, all the things I don't have, and will never have."

"I know I failed you, Kenzie, up to now at least. But don't you understand? Every step we take gets us closer to the life you envision."

"We'll never see that life, Erroll. Especially the children. Look at us. We're both thirty years old and haven't had so much as a false alarm. Even if we somehow make it back to the US, we're too old to succeed there. We left when we were five and only kids. If we get back, we'll be thirty and old. Poppa died at age fifty-four, so we're pretty far into the last halves of our lives."

"I'm sorry, Kenzie. I tried and will never stop trying. We'll walk slower tomorrow. We don't care how long it takes to get to Glasgow. There's no deadline and things will be better when we get there, I promise."

"You can't promise, Erroll. You don't know what the future holds, any more than I do. You always think prosperity and happiness are around the next corner. They aren't."

"Not yet for prosperity. But happiness is purely inside our minds. You've made me wonderfully happy, Kenzie, and I'm sorry I haven't done the same for you. But we gotta get to Glasgow. Don't you believe that?"

"Erroll, I didn't mean you haven't made me happy because you have. All the same, I'm kind of melancholy. But yes, I want to go to Glasgow as much as you do, although I wish you could realize it might be something we can't do."

"Again, I'm sorry, Kenzie. We'll slow the pace tomorrow, and if this wood stays with us, we can camp almost anywhere. We'll rest today, start late tomorrow, and do a shorter walk then."

"I don't want to hold us up, but I'm worn out. Maybe I'll be better in the morning."

"I hope you are, but it doesn't matter, because we'll slow down." They didn't walk more that afternoon, but Erroll made a fire and roasted two potatoes. He insisted Kenzie eat both. He counted the potatoes in the gunnysack and found sixteen.

Erroll awoke first the next morning, and didn't directly wake Kenzie, but made noise as he built a fire. He roasted one potato for Kenzie and said he wasn't hungry. He made only a small fire, due to a calm wind, and put the fire out when he finished, to avoid a smoke plume.

Kenzie ate her potato and apologized. "I'm sorry I turned into such a sorehead yesterday, Erroll. I don't know what came over me."

"I know what came over you—you had a fit of realism. I understand it all, and we'll take it a little easier today."

"I can go for that. Did you look at the map?"

"Yes, we did yesterday, and planned our route to Spean Bridge. We won't get that far today, and don't need to plan that part again."

Erroll walked in front as always, but walked slower. They continued until about noon again, saw a young rabbit again, and ate berries in a wild dewberry patch once more, but didn't reach Spean Bridge. They camped in thick woods, and Kenzie asked, "How far do you think it is to Spean Bridge?"

"I don't know for sure. Maybe five or more km. We'll probably get there tomorrow."

"I wish I hadn't spilled out all my feelings yesterday, Erroll. I might have made you think I wish I'd married somebody else, but nothing could be further from the truth. I feel so much better today, and so much more optimistic, I won't talk that way again."

"Hush, Kenzie. I'm gonna take better care of you, and you're gonna have all that stuff you talked about, except perhaps the children. That part might be unrealistic."

"You'd better eat a potato today, because if you don't, I'll chase you all the way down the hill into the loch!"

"I'm tempted to see if you'll do it." Erroll grinned.

"You'd better not!"

Erroll didn't roast potatoes immediately, but went out to look for another young rabbit, found one, ran it down, and cooked it over the same fire with two potatoes.

After they ate, Kenzie remarked, "I feel comfortably full. I might take a nap."

"Me too. I'll put the fire out first and gather up some leaves to sleep on."

They slept a couple hours, and then talked and joked until after dark. When they returned to their leaf pile for the evening they slept all night, but awakened at first light. Kenzie asked her usual question. "Should we look at the map?"

"Yes, we have two bridges coming up, and we should get across the first today." Erroll removed the map from the jar and again touched the map with his finger. "If we cross the first one at Spean Bridge the next one's about fifteen to twenty km farther, at a place called Fort William. We mustn't try for Fort William today."

"How far is the first one?"

"I don't know exactly, but it's under eight km. You ready to go?"

"I'm ready."

They walked more, and stopped yet again for wild dewberries. The road turned mostly east toward Spean Bridge, and they came out of the woods not far from the bridge they needed to cross. Kenzie looked down the hill toward the road. "We haven't seen Dal for a while. Perhaps he gave up and went back to Inverness. Do you think?"

"He might have, but I'm afraid to count on it. We need to be as careful as always about bridges."

"Won't it be easier to walk farther on the road, more than just over the bridge? What if we put our disguises on like we always do, you look, and if you don't see a problem, we walk separately like we always do, but get on the road sooner and stay on it longer?"

"I don't know, Kenzie. Every meter we walk on the road could bring us closer to disaster."

"You can do what you want. I'm going to stay on the road longer."

"So will I, then. Get off on the east side and I'll get off where you do."

They changed their appearance, and Erroll went to the edge of the road to look. He came back, looking upset. "The sorrels are down there, Kenzie. We have to go back and stay in the woods again." They returned and remained in their camp all day and all night.

While waiting in the camp, Kenzie raised an issue with Erroll. "You said you'd read the Bible to me every day. You did until we started this trip, and since then you haven't read it to me one time."

"I'll make it all up today, Kenzie. How many days have we missed?"

"I don't know, probably at least a week."

"We must read thirty-five minutes today then, if we make up five minutes a day."

"That sounds awfully precise, Erroll. Will it hurt to read for thirty-six minutes?"

"You want thirty-six?"

"I want something spontaneous and unplanned."

"We can't do it that way, Kenzie. If we don't plan it, we won't do it."

"Whatever you think. Where did you leave off last time?"

"We left off at the end of a section called Acts."

"So what's next?"

"How can I know? I'll look." Erroll unbuttoned the new pocket on his shirt, took the Bible out, and removed the oilpaper. He discovered the part after Acts is called Romans, started at the beginning of it, and read all the way through that section, to the end of chapter sixteen. A Eureka moment struck him near the middle of the part he read, and he asked a preliminary question about it after he stopped. "Do you think I'm perfect, Kenzie?"

"That's a stupid question, Erroll. Nobody's perfect, but you're pretty close."

"No, I mean do you think God looks at me and thinks I'm perfect?"

"I don't know what God thinks. Maybe, maybe not."

"I know I'm not, and you know I'm not. Did you notice, not even the guy writing Romans saw himself as perfect? Did you catch the part where he said he couldn't understand why he didn't do the good he wanted to do, but instead did the bad he didn't want to do? Doesn't that sound a lot like me or you?"

"I never thought about it, Erroll. Perhaps. I don't know."

"It does, Kenzie. So that calls to mind stuff the writer said earlier in what we read today. He said straight out nobody's perfect, but God can make us the same as if we are. Do you see it as exciting that even people as bad as we are, can be the same as perfect?"

"You sure got a lot of crazy things out of that stuff. Maybe you shouldn't read it any more."

"You might think it's crazy, and I'll not bother you with it—for a while. But wait until we get on that ship, where you can't get away from me!"

"You still think we'll make it to Glasgow?"

"We must, Kenzie. If we don't, we'll waste perfectly good ship tickets. We can't do that now, can we?"

"Put the Bible back in your pocket, Erroll, and act normal."

Chapter 24

1912

Erroll returned the Bible to his pocket and looked for a young rabbit he could catch, but didn't find one. They rested all day and awoke the next morning ready to go. They didn't eat breakfast, but donned their disguises and approached the road by the bridge again. Erroll went ahead and looked. "I don't see anything today."

Kenzie stepped onto the road immediately, and Erroll followed about fifty meters behind. They crossed the bridge, went about a hundred meters more, and Kenzie left the road on the east side. Erroll joined her there in a few minutes and whispered, "Did you see the horse forty or fifty meters south from here? That's a McCarty horse."

"I saw it. That's why I left the road. I hope nobody spotted us, and Dal's not about to haul us back to Inverness."

"Me too, but we have to wait and see. According to the liveryman, if Dal himself didn't see us we're all right."

"What can we do, Erroll?"

"Nothing, except walk away from here. You ready?"

"Let's go."

"I hope we can walk a little more than half way to Fort William before we camp, but if you get tired, Kenzie, we can stop anywhere we find a good spot."

"Let's go."

They walked at a slow pace and came to a cornfield, which safely hid them. Erroll asked, "Do you think we can eat some of this corn and not be guilty of stealing?"

"Erroll, the corn won't be ripe until fall."

"Yes, but look under the shucks. The grains are filled out, and they're juicy. Look what happens when I pop one with my thumbnail."

"Corn's hog feed isn't it, Erroll?"

"Yes, but people can eat it too. We did it one winter after you bought corn meal."

"I suppose you're right."

"Do you think we'll be thieves if we eat some, Kenzie?"

"You mean if we eat hog feed?"

"If we eat corn."

Kenzie grinned. "I bet this field is for hogs. Smell'em? I don't think we're thieves if we eat hog feed."

"That's what I hoped you'd say. Let's see who can eat the most."

They ate two ears apiece, and then Erroll extended his earlier question. "Do you think we'll be thieves if we put some of this in the gunnysack to cook over a fire later?"

"Of course."

"Oh. Then we can't do it."

"Of course not."

They ate more corn, walked farther, and stopped about noon in some trees at the edge of a pasture and near a stream. Kenzie inquired, "How far is it to Fort William?"

"I don't know, but surely not more than sixteen or eighteen km. We won't get there tomorrow, but the map shows another bridge there."

"We haven't seen Dal today. You think he gave up?"

"Beats me. Perhaps nobody saw us when we saw the horse, or maybe they went somewhere to wait for us. We should look on the bright side and enjoy our trip. If they get us later, we'll have fun until then."

"That's what I love about you, Erroll. You have fun, and I have fun when you're around."

Erroll grinned and took up the 'fun' mantle. "What do you want for lunch? We have potatoes and . . . potatoes."

"I think I'll choose a potato this time, Erroll. How about you?"

"I'll have the same. I'll make a fire, but a small one, and put it out when the potatoes are cooked, because if Dal saw us back at the bridge, he might look for smoke. I think I'll cook two of'em for each of us." Erroll took the potatoes out of the gunnysack, and then counted. They lounged the entire afternoon, and talked about the pleasant pasture view. Kenzie cleared a smooth place to sleep, and they used it early, but awakened early.

Erroll talked first about the map the next morning. "We don't need to check the map today, because all we plan to do is go on toward Fort William. We won't make it all the way, so we don't have to worry about the bridge there."

"We're ready to go then, aren't we?"

"Yep. We're ready."

Erroll picked up the gunnysack and they walked. They went through mostly open country that day, and walked farther away from the road. They ate corn in another field, but didn't see wild fruit or young rabbits. They walked across terrain more level than they did earlier, and made more progress than usual, but saw a mountain ahead. They camped near the base of it, and Kenzie inquired, "How far do you think we are from Fort William?"

"Maybe we should look at the map. I didn't notice that mountain before, but it very likely shows on the map." Erroll hauled the map out of the gunnysack, unfolded it, and pointed. "Yes, there's the mountain. We're well over halfway to Fort William. It looks like the bridge is on the other side of the mountain."

"Do we really have to go over that thing, Erroll?"

"We're pretty well worn out and we don't have much to eat. I don't know if we can."

"You surely don't plan to walk around it?"

"No, that could be worse than going over it, Kenzie. Maybe we can do our disguise thing and cross the road. Perhaps we can walk between the road and the loch. But that'll be for tomorrow. Let's rest and eat potatoes today. You want two or one?"

"I want ten! But how many do we have?"

"We have nine, an odd number. How about if you have two and I have one, to leave us with six?"

"You're as hungry as I am. We should each eat a whole one and then split one."

"Not a chance. I'll cook three, and force a second one on you later."

Kenzie did indeed eat two potatoes, and Erroll one. They took another afternoon nap, went to sleep for the evening without more food, and started the next morning without breakfast. They adopted their disguises and walked directly west down the hill to the road.

They approached the road, and Kenzie exclaimed, "I can see the loch barely on the other side of the road! We can't walk there."

"You're right. I don't want to even think about walking on the road, but maybe we should, until we get over the bridge. That'll be a long walk—maybe ten or eleven km. You think we can get away with it?"

"Erroll, I'm so tired and hungry it doesn't matter to me any more. If you think it's the best way I'm for it, but do we have to walk apart?"

"Maybe not. Let's walk on the far left side of the road, and if Dal comes past, we can hope we see him before he sees us, jump off to the left, and fall down."

"I like the fall down idea, Erroll, but do we have to wait for Dal to go past?" She grinned.

"Be serious, Kenzie." He grinned too. They walked, went faster than they expected, crossed the bridge south of Fort William safely, saw many houses, and walked among people there.

Kenzie whispered, "All these people make me nervous. Somebody's sure to recognize us."

Erroll whispered back, "Who knows us in Fort William? We're less conspicuous walking where other people walk than when we're the only people around. Maybe fortune smiled on us today, and if true, so be it; we'll take as much luck as possible. I think it'll work to walk on the road again tomorrow all the way to the edge of town, so you'll have easier walking."

"Let's wait to talk about it, Erroll."

"There's some trees; let's camp over there."

"Don't you think we should camp farther out of town?"

"No this looks fine to me." They went among the trees, but didn't build a fire. They each ate a raw potato, and they took a nap. Kenzie woke while Erroll remained asleep, and saw the sun high in the sky.

She awakened him. "Erroll. Erroll. We're like squirrels in a bare tree here. Do you think we can walk to the edge of town and find a more private place to camp?"

"What? Give me a minute to wake up. If you want to go, I do too." Erroll sat a few seconds, stood, put the gunnysack over his shoulder, they went back to the road, and walked more than an hour. They came to a remote wooded spot and Erroll inquired, "You wanta camp here?"

"Yes, this looks like a better place than where we were." They stopped, and Erroll explored for several minutes, while Kenzie used a forked tree limb to sweep a place clean to sleep.

Erroll returned and informed, "I found a wild plum tree on the back side of these trees. Come on."

Kenzie went, they ate all the plums they could, then Erroll picked more, and put them in his hat to take back to the camp for breakfast the next morning. They didn't build a fire, but went to sleep. They woke up before sunrise the next morning, ate their plums, and sat for several minutes.

Kenzie suggested a look at the map and asked, "Do you think we're halfway yet?"

After he found the map, Erroll replied. "No, not yet, but we should hit that mark in only a few more days." He pointed to the map and explained, "Here's where we are. It looks like the next bridge is at Ballachulish, and it might be a long one. It's probably thirty or more km away, and we can already see hills or mountains up ahead. We could be looking at a tough two or three day walk."

"We don't usually have breakfast, and I enjoyed it. Perhaps we can walk farther today."

"Maybe. You ready to start, Kenzie?"

"Whenever you are."

Erroll grabbed the gunnysack and they walked south. They walked more than an hour, but the hills steadily worsened, and they could see even higher climbs ahead. When they reached the top of the third or fourth hill, he asked, "How are you holding up?"

She panted a moment. "I'm all out of breath."

"Let's stop and rest." They stopped, Kenzie caught her breath, and Erroll proposed, "Maybe we should stop, even though we haven't gone far today. What do you think?"

"The road we walked on yesterday was so-oo nice. What if we walk on it again until we get past these hills?"

"We don't know how far that will be, Kenzie, and we'll take a big chance."

"I'm so worn out and we have so little food, it could take us days to get through these hills."

"You think it'll work to keep on like we are until we get to a low spot and it's time to start uphill again? From there we can turn west toward the road, and when we almost reach it, we can creep up to it and look. If we don't see trouble, then maybe I can agree to put on our disguises and walk on the road, because unless we do, we won't travel far today. We can stay by the east edge of the road like we did in Fort William, stay alert, and be ready to get off the road." They adopted Erroll's plan, came to the road, walked on it toward Ballachulish, and according to the map, traveled almost thirty km before they stopped. They camped for the night outside a town that turned out to be North Ballachulish, made a fire, and roasted the last of their potatoes.

Erroll went alone to find the bridge early the next morning. He came back in about an hour, and reported bad news. "I talked to some people in town. They say Loch Leven is the barrier and a ferry is the way across it, so I went down toward it, and saw Dal standing on the ferry dock. I talked to some other guys, and one of them told me McCarty people came two days ago, and rented space in a tavern. Dal may plan to stay here for a while. The loch's too big for us to wade or swim, so all I can think to do is out-wait Dal, and hope we don't starve."

"You sure you saw Dal?"

"Complete with rifle."

"You think he'll stay more than a day?"

"I don't know, but I'm afraid he will."

"What if I go to the ferry alone and let him catch me and start back to Inverness with me? I only hold you back anyway, and you can escape, ride the ferry, go on to Glasgow, and wait to see if I show up."

"Kenzie, that's silly. We don't know what Dal might do if he captures you, and even if you escape somewhere, we'll be in as bad a shape as we're in now; worse, because neither of us will know where the other is."

"You have a better plan?"

"Let's walk east along Loch Leven. The map doesn't show a way across except for the ferry here, but maybe we'll find another ferry or a shallow place or something."

"If you say so, Erroll." She turned away. "We'll die soon anyway, and the north side of the loch is as good a place to do it as any other."

"Kenzie! We won't die soon. We'll make it to Glasgow and we'll leave every single McCarty memory behind."

"When will we get there, Erroll?"

"I don't know. But you gotta believe we will, because we will. You ready to start?"

"If you insist."

They walked in silence on a ridge far above the north shore of

Loch Leven until mid-morning, when Erroll held up his right hand and stopped. "I see a house or something up ahead."

"Can't we just go around it?"

"Maybe we can, but look down at the loch. You see that boat down there?"

Kenzie looked mildly excited for the first time in days. "Yes! I see it! I wonder if the boat goes with the house?"

"I don't know. You have any ideas about what we should do next?"

Kenzie's interested look faded, but returned. "Is it too risky to knock on the door of the house and ask for a boat ride?"

"Yes, I think it's risky, but" Erroll paused, and then adopted a playful tone, "we're desperate aren't we?"

"Yes we are. Do you think only one of us should go up to the house, or should we both go?"

"We're together, Kenzie. Let's both go." They made their way to the house and then to a door facing the loch. Erroll set the gunnysack down, hesitated, crossed the fingers on his left hand, tensed his shoulders, and knocked with his right hand.

Chapter 25

1912

A ruddy-faced woman older than Kenzie answered the knock; tiny sweat droplets covered her upper lip. She stood in the doorway and didn't speak, so Erroll did. "We're Erroll and Kenzie Paterson. Is that your boat down at the edge of the loch?"

The woman didn't question Erroll's curiosity, but merely smiled and answered, "Yes, 'tis. Ye 'ave need for it?"

Erroll replied, "Do we ever. You want to know why?"

The woman smiled again. "Ah don't need to know why, but if ye want me t' know, Ah'll listen."

Erroll and Kenzie told the woman their entire story. They interrupted each other often, but left nothing out. The woman smiled yet again and said, "Burt—that's ma 'usband—'e'll be 'ere 'round noon, and 'e'll row ye acrost after we eat. Ye gotta eat afore ye go. Ye're nothin' but skin and bones, and while we wait, ye need a bath. Ah'll dip some water out of th' barrel out back, and Ah've a'ready got a 'ot teakettle. Come on in."

They entered the house and felt the heat from a fire in the cook stove. The woman showed them both rooms of her house. "This 'ere's th' kitchen, and th' other room there's th' sittin' room and bedroom. We got a big tub in there, big enough for th' both o' ye. Soon as Ah put th' water in it, ye can get your clothes off and soak a spell. Ah'll pull th' blanket acrost the door 'ere, and won't come in while ye're in th' bath."

Kenzie accepted before Erroll could decline. "Thank you Mrs. . . ."

"That'd be Mrs. Bradley. Mrs. Burt Bradley. Call me Thelma."

"Thank you Thelma. We know we need a bath, because we've walked for days, but food sounds best of all. We're pretty hungry."

"I can tell by lookin' at ye young'uns ye're hungry. We'll take care o' that when Burt gets back, but look at your clothes. They're 'bout tore off ye. Mine and Burt's clothes'll be a little loose on ye, but Ah'll find some o' ours ye can put on after your bath. Ah'll make chicken nests out o' those ye got on now."

Erroll crowded a few words into the monologue. "Mrs. Bradley, we're grateful for your hospitality, and we accept all of it except the clothes. We can't let you do that."

"Quiet, boy. Ah ain't Mrs. nobody. Ah a'ready telt ye Ah'm Thelma. Your missus knows ye need clothes, and there's no point in takin' a bath if ye put those tore-up rags back on. Right Kenzie?"

Kenzie nodded and shot a begging look at Erroll. Erroll replied, "We'll take them if you insist, but we want to know how to mail money to you. I don't know when we can pay, but we will when we can."

"Quiet, boy. Ain't ye lern't t' respect your elders? Ah'll tell ye 'ow t' write t' us, 'cause Ah'll not feel good 'till I 'ear ye're safe where ye're 'eaded, but don't never think ye need t' send money."

Thelma put clean clothes for both of them on the bed, and went out to get water. Erroll followed. "Can I carry that for you, Thelma?"

"Ye sure can. Ma back's been actin' up somethin' fierce lately." Erroll carried three buckets of water to pour in the tub. Mrs. Bradley dumped in a full teakettle of hot water, draped a towel and washcloth over the edge of the tub, and dropped a bar of lye soap into it. She went back in the kitchen and pulled the blanket across the door. The Patersons scrubbed until they felt cleaner than they could remember. They stepped out of the tub, dried off, put on the Bradley's clothes, and went back into the kitchen.

Kenzie asked, "May I help you, Thelma?"

"No, Ah got 't under control 'ere."

"May I set the table then? I think it's great Erroll and I can sit on chairs at a real table and eat out of real plates. We haven't done that for a while."

"Sure, set th' table. Dishes 's in th' pie safe over there, and forks 's on th' end o' th' table."

Kenzie set the table, and then Thelma shooed both Patersons outside; she said they'd feel cooler there. They found a cleared-off area east of the house with a log along one side of it to sit on. They looked out over the loch, admired the view, and Kenzie stretched her arms over her head. "I was filthy and worn out when we came here, but that bath pepped me up. I feel almost like I want to feel. All I need now is food, and I can hardly wait."

"Right, same here. About these different clothes, maybe if I change my hat—smear mud on it? —and if you change your bonnet—dewberry juice? —we won't need any other disguise. The country looks awful rough to walk on around here, but maybe we can walk on the road in these different clothes."

"I don't see why not, except the gunnysack will be a dead giveaway."

"Maybe I can ditch it. These clothes are so big I can put stuff in the pockets, and we don't have much left in the gunnysack anyway."

"You did take Poppa's Bible out of your old clothes before Thelma carried them away, didn't you?"

"I took everything out of all the old pockets. I'm sure there's plenty of room in these pockets for the stuff in the gunnysack."

"I wish Mr. Bradley would hurry up. Now that I anticipate food, I don't want to wait another minute."

"If he's going by the sun, Kenzie, he won't be here for a while."

They almost gave up on Mr. Bradley. Erroll noted, "We're not moving, but I'm so comfortable here it doesn't seem to matter."

A man eventually approached the house from the west. Thelma came out and talked to him before he entered. She stood with her back to the Patersons, waved her arms a lot, and after a time, turned around and invited, "Come on in t' eat, young'uns. This 'ere's Burton, ma 'usband."

All four people went in to the biggest and best meal the Patersons could remember, even bigger and better than Tiny Kirk wagon meals. They ate all the way to their full-and-can't-hold-any-more point, and then Thelma pressured them to eat more. When they couldn't, Thelma addressed her husband, "Ye better take these young'uns acrost th' loch Burt, and tell'em what ye telt me."

Burt cleared his throat. "Ah chust got back from talkin' t' ma brother James in North Ballachulish. 'E's goin' t' Glasgow tomorrow. 'E 'as a 'orse and a buggy, and 'e expects t' make it in a day. After I row ye acrost th' loch, Ah'll go back there this afternoon and tell'im about ye. Ah got a food stand aside th' road south o' th' loch, and if ye'll wait there 'till 'e comes by, 'e'll stop for ye. Ah think ye can ride beside him in th' buggy, and nobody'll look at ye."

Erroll swallowed hard and tried to speak, but temporarily failed. When he could almost talk, he choked, but eventually said, "Mr. Bradley, I don't know how we can ever thank you. We were going to make it, but it will be so much easier this way. We're indebted to you, and we don't know how we can pay you back."

"Ah ain't Mr. nobody to ye, Ah'm Burt. Don't worry 'bout 't. Ah know ye'd do the same for me if I 'uz in your country. Chust do 't for somebody and Ah'll be paid. Now let's go down t' that boat."

They went down the hill to the edge of the loch, and Burt took them across. "Good bye and good luck t' ye. Th' road runs alongside th' loch, and's close. Go due south t' find ma food stand. Ah'll go now." Then he turned the boat north, and rowed away.

They walked rapidly, but stopped soon when they saw the road with the food stand where Burt told them. They made a camp, added the mud and dewberry juice to their hat and bonnet, and retired early to their leaf pile. They didn't sleep well, but they slept some, and awakened at first light. They hurried to the food stand and waited perhaps two hours before a buggy stopped. Erroll asked, "Are you Mr. Bradley?"

"That'd be me, or better, chust call me James. Ye Mr. Paterson?"

Erroll ignored Kenzie's grin. "That's right . . . Erroll, and this is Kenzie. You going to Glasgow?"

"That'd be right. Come on up."

Erroll helped Kenzie up, climbed up beside her, and James resumed his travel. Erroll checked another point. "Where in Glasgow you going?"

"Ah'm 'eaded t' Admore Road by th' water, 'bout a km from the ferry. Ah got a wee package t' deliver, but Burt told me ye'll be wantin' the ferry acrost River Clyde, so I'll take ye down there."

Erroll looked at Kenzie but didn't say anything, so Kenzie replied, "Oh no, Mr. Bradley. We walked so awfully far, another km will seem like nothing. Don't take us, we'll walk."

"Hush your talk girl. Ah'll take ye, and ye cain't stop me!"

Erroll responded, "Thank you Mr. Bradley. We owe you and your brother more than you can ever know."

"Ye don't owe me nuthin'. We Scots chust do this. This ain't th' first time Ah 'elped somebody out, and 'twon't be th' last. People 'elped me a bunch o' times too. Don't worry 'bout 't."

James continued to drive, far out east over a spectacular mountain pass, then south toward Glasgow. He stopped the buggy when the sun reached its peak in the sky, went to the back, untied a bucket, brought it to the front, climbed back up in the buggy seat, and resumed driving. He pointed a thumb toward the bucket, and told Kenzie, "Ma wife made sandwiches and put milk in bottles. She made 'nough for us all. Fish 'round in this 'ere bucket and see what she put in 't."

Kenzie looked, and found six steak sandwiches, plus three jelly sandwiches, and three bottles of milk. "Mr. Bradley, we can't eat all this."

"We cain't if we don't start. Get yourself a sandwich and get one for Erroll and me. Dig in."

Except for bathroom stops, James drove continuously all afternoon long and they ate sandwiches until mid-afternoon. James ate both his steak sandwiches, plus the jelly, but the Patersons saved one steak sandwich each. They put the two remaining sandwiches in Erroll's pocket, because they left the gunnysack back at their camp south of Loch Leven. They arrived at the ferry dock in late afternoon. James stopped the buggy and announced, "We're 'ere."

Erroll and Kenzie jumped down off the buggy, and Erroll turned to thank James, but saw only the back of the buggy move away, so he yelled, "Thanks James."

Erroll turned to Kenzie, grinned, and commented, "All we need is to see Dal on the ferry when it comes."

"You think it can't happen, Erroll?"

"Naw, I don't think it'll happen. Dal's still looking for us up at Loch Leven."

"I hope you're right, but we'll never be sure until we're on a ship moving out to sea. You have our money?"

"All that's left after I bought the map in Inverness. It should be plenty to pay for two ferry tickets."

"Let's buy them and then mingle with the other people, to make it harder for Dal to see us if he's on the ferry."

"Kenzie, you're silly."

"You said that before about Dal, and who turned out to be silly?"

"I did then, but I won't this time."

"Let's be careful, just in case."

"Whatever you think. It's as easy to mingle as to not mingle." Erroll bought the tickets, and they hobnobbed with other people for almost an hour before the ferry arrived. They scrutinized the people getting off and didn't see Dal. They waited to get on the ferry until they could do it with a group of people, and then waited several more minutes before the ferry crossed over to the south.

Kenzie again warned on the way over, "I know you think it's silly, but I don't want Dal to shoot you, ever, not at Inverness, and not at Glasgow. We need to watch for him, and if he's here, we need to see him first."

"Kenzie, I told him we're going to Glasgow. I didn't say where in Glasgow."

"Even Dumb Dal can figure out there's no particular reason for us to go to Glasgow except to get on a ship."

"Maybe, Kenzie. We can watch, but I don't expect to see anything." The ferry docked on the south of the river, the Glasgow Port side. They walked off it in a crowd of other people. Erroll noted, "I don't see Dal, and neither do I see a ship."

"There's a big dock. One of those guys over there probably knows about the ship."

"You wait here. I'll go over and check into it." Erroll went and returned. "They say that's the spot, but the ship from the US won't be here for at least a couple days, more if the weather's been bad out on the Atlantic. They say it carries freight as well as passengers, will stay here two days after it arrives, and will stop at Moville before it heads back to the US. We probably need to find a place around here we can camp for two or three days."

"That might be a good plan, Erroll, but I think we should check back here every day just in case those guys are wrong."

"We might as well check, because we don't have anything else to do." Erroll looked up and down the river. "I don't know where we can camp, but we should find a place before it gets dark."

Chapter 26

1912

"Yes, we should, and I looked around. How about up in those trees?" Kenzie pointed to some trees up the hill south.

"Looks good as any to me."

They walked toward a wood about eight hundred meters away and went about forty meters into it. Erroll commented, "We don't need a fire tonight, because we had a good noon meal. And I have sandwiches in my pocket. Those should hold us two days easy enough."

"Do we have any money?"

"We're down to not much after I bought the ferry tickets, but we might be able to afford something. Maybe we can look for a grocery store on day three and see what we can find, but tonight we can sleep good and sleep late, because even if the ship shows up tonight we know it'll be there all day tomorrow."

"Can you look for a rabbit or for plums or something?"

"Yeah I can, but let's wait until tomorrow. I don't need more food now, do you?"

"No, tomorrow'll be fine."

They cleared off a place, piled up some leaves for a bed, and were almost asleep when a bunch of cattle wandered into their camp. Kenzie jumped up and asked, "Will they step on us?"

"I don't know, but let's don't wait to find out. I'll see if I can drive them away." Erroll waved his arms, but told Kenzie he didn't want to yell at the cattle, because he didn't want to attract attention. The cattle meandered slowly back and forth, but gradually moved on, and the Patersons tried to rest again. They didn't fall asleep for a while, but they slept later than usual the next morning.

They scheduled no travel or activity for the day. They ate both their sandwiches for breakfast, and talked. Kenzie recalled, "You remember, Erroll, I said you always see prosperity and happiness around the next corner, but it's never there? I could not've been more wrong about the happiness part, because we indeed found it, and I didn't see it until it hit us. I didn't foresee the Bradleys, and I still can't believe they helped us so much. If we had to walk all the way, we'd only be about halfway, we'd still have a lot of bridges to cross, and we'd be really hungry now. But we may have to wait for another corner to see the prosperity part!"

"Yes, I can't believe what the Bradleys did either. I wish we could do something in exchange."

"We can't, Erroll, so we need to forget about it. I can see the ship dock from here and it's still empty, so maybe we don't need to go down there today."

"Yes, I can see it too, Kenzie. But that means we have a long boring day coming up."

Kenzie grinned, and launched an abstruse line of questions. "You remember you said up north of Loch Leven, happiness is in our minds?"

"Yep, Kenzie, and it is."

"And do you remember you said today'll be boring?"

"Yep. Do you see it different?"

"Yes! If happiness is in our minds, why not boring? We don't have to be bored unless we choose to be."

Erroll laughed. "Kenzie, you're silly."

"I might be silly, but you know I'm right."

"So explain it to me. What'll happen today to blow my boredom away?"

"I'm about to happen to you Erroll! I bet you can't keep me away from you."

"So are you about to chase me, or what?"

"I'm not merely 'about' to chase you—I'll catch you and tickle you until you're silly too."

"I still think you're the silly one, Kenzie."

"I'm coming after you now. If you don't run, you'll be easy pick-in's." Kenzie ran at Erroll, and he ran from her, but she caught him when he stumbled over a vine. She proved more than able to dispel boredom; she and Erroll tickled each other off and on for the entire day.

Night came, they returned to their pile of leaves, and went to sleep. They awakened in the morning, and Kenzie moved close to Erroll. She murmured, "Erroll, I want to talk seriously to you."

He affected a look of terror, and replied, "You can't catch me to-day. I'll hide behind a tree and wait until it's over."

Kenzie grinned, but persisted. "No, I have things on my mind—three things, and I want you to know about them."

Erroll exchanged his terror-stricken look for a smile. "Maybe I can't beat you to a tree anyway. What's on your mind?"

"You remember that day back in the woods north of Spean Bridge when you read the Bible to me?"

Erroll nodded.

"Do you remember I said maybe you shouldn't read it anymore?"

Erroll nodded again.

"I meant it then, but I feel a hundred per cent different now. Do you suppose it's because our prospects are better now?"

Erroll looked thoughtful, and eventually replied, "I'm glad you see it different, but I don't think how you feel has anything to do with it. Do you remember when Poppa read to us years ago about some guy who said Jesus strengthened him whether he was full or hungry?"

"No, Erroll, I don't remember that."

"He did read it, and I think it's true for us too. You didn't bring all this up merely so I won't pester you about it on the ship like I said I would, did you?" He grinned, and lightly slapped her leg.

"No, Erroll. But what I mean to say is that even though I didn't appreciate it for a few days, I'm glad you went ahead and read to me every day. And there's another thing I want to tell you."

"What is it, Kenzie?"

"I'm truly grateful you didn't let me give up back by Invergarry. I saw little chance we could survive, but you rightly insisted we go on. I love you for that, and for everything else, Erroll, and that's the third thing. I love you and I'm going to kiss you now." She kissed Erroll repeatedly. He responded with enthusiasm.

Chapter 27

1912

A ship docked late that afternoon where Kenzie and Erroll expected their ship to arrive. They talked more as they walked down the hill toward the ship. "Kenzie, on the off chance you're right and Dal's snooping around, you walk in front, pull your bonnet down, and get on first. I'll find your ticket." Erroll looked in his pockets, drew the tickets out, and gave one to Kenzie.

She accepted the ticket with questions. "You think these tickets'll work? You think old Cecil gave us real ones?"

"If they don't work, Kenzie, we went through a lot for nothing."

Kenzie noted, "Our name isn't on these tickets anywhere. If they're good, maybe we should be Jim and Jane MacDonald just in case Dal looks for us."

"I said it before, Kenzie. You're silly."

"All right, I'm silly. Do you mind being Jim MacDonald?"

"I don't guess so."

"Then that's who you are. I'm Jane MacDonald until we're out of port."

They came to the ship, boarded one after the other, and didn't see Dal. Erroll laughed aloud. "We made it, Kenzie! Our tickets worked, we're on the ship, and Dal didn't find us."

"Perhaps we made it, Jim. Don't forget who we are. Non-passengers can come and go almost up to departure time. The ticket-taker told me we have a second-class room on the second deck, and after we find it, I think we should look for an inconspicuous place up above where we can see who comes aboard, and watch for Dal."

"If we must. Let's compare room numbers; it'll be nice if we're in the same one."

"You're in twenty-one, right, Jim?"

"Yes, Jane. Let's find it."

The 'MacDonalds' found their room, and went back up to the top deck to watch. They didn't see Dal, and when somebody told them it was dinnertime, they went below deck again to a cafeteria, to have their first actual meal since the buggy ride with James. Soon after they found a place to sit, Kenzie gasped, "Look."

"At what?"

"On second thought don't look, but I see a polis officer. He's behind you, talking to the captain. Don't turn around."

"How do you know he's a polis officer?"

"He's wearing a uniform with a patch that says, 'Strathclyde Polis'."

"Is he looking at us?"

"No, he's showing a paper to the captain."

"Is the captain looking at us?"

"No, he's shaking his head no. Aren't you glad we didn't board as who we really are?"

Erroll noticed people looking at them. "Shh." He put his finger on his lips and whispered, "What now?"

Kenzie whispered back, "The officer may be leaving." She remained quiet a moment. "He is leaving . . . he's gone. Oh, no!"

"What?"

"The captain's coming."

Erroll continued to whisper. "Act normal."

Kenzie sighed with relief. "He stopped. He's talking to someone."

"Act normal. He still might come here."

The ship's captain walked toward the 'MacDonalds' again, and continued past them. Erroll exulted, "We made it now! Dal doesn't know we're here! We're on the way!"

"Perhaps. But this ship won't leave tonight, and maybe not tomorrow. And we have a stop in Moville, you know. Dal's people might wait for us there."

"Kenzie, you know they won't. He doesn't know we came here to get on a ship and even if he somehow discovers it, he can't know which ship."

"You think he might travel to Moville on this ship, and be on board with us, however long it takes to get there?"

"No, Kenzie. You're imagining Dal knows things he can't know."

"I hope you're right. Do you remember Dal's hat?"

"No, I don't, Kenzie."

"I do. I'll look for that hat over every group I see until we're under way out of Moville."

"People are standing in line for food. Let's join them."

They enjoyed a meal, and then went inside their room and closed the door. Erroll commented, "I don't mind sleeping on the ground sometimes, but I expect to like sleeping on a bed too. Except for that time at the McDowell's—and I don't consider their couch a real bed—tonight'll be my first night to sleep with you on a real bed. A bed and you too! If I could see Dal, I'd brag a bit!"

"Erroll, you don't want to see Dal. I'm not sure we completely gave him the slip, but we made progress. Surely the captain won't let him look in passenger rooms. And besides that, perhaps the polis don't have authority on a ship. You think?"

"Yes, you might be right, Kenzie."

"I'm Jane, remember?"

"How long must we do that . . . Jane?"

"Let's stay MacDonalds until we leave Moville. And we're probably on some kind of captain's list as MacDonalds, so officially we have to stick with it until we get off the ship."

"Speaking of getting off the ship, Jane, do you think we'll have to prove we're US citizens?"

"I have no idea Jim—shh. I hear footsteps outside."The sound of footsteps came closer, went past, and receded. Kenzie resumed. "I have no idea, Jim. But we can do it, because the certificates that say we're Scottish citizens say we're American too. And it's on our wedding certificate. Those are in the jar in your pocket." Kenzie paused again. "I wonder how long it will take to get to New York after we leave Moville?"

"I asked the guys at the dock. They said seven to ten days from Glasgow, depending on weather."

"Who's watching McCarty's cattle while Dal chases us, Jim?"

"If it's like after I got fired, nobody. Dal and Unc. thought it real important when I did it, but nobody seems to care about it now, Jane."

"I wonder if Uncle Eric knows Dal's off chasing us?"

"Probably. Dal has the carriage and four horses, plus the liveryman and the butler. How can he not know, Jane?"

"You sleepy, Jim?"

"Yeah, Jane."

"I'll try out this bunk with you, but I can tell you right now, Jim, you ain't no Erroll!"

They turned in. Their room had no windows so the sun didn't tell them when morning came, but instead a loud scraping sound from above told them. They awoke suddenly, and Kenzie asked, "What's that?"

"I don't know." Erroll opened the door slightly and looked at John's watch. "It's nearly 7:30. Maybe we heard freight scrape against the ship."

"Do you know when they have breakfast here, Jim?"

"Let's go to the cafeteria and wait, Jane."

They went to the cafeteria about eight, and learned breakfast ended an hour earlier. Kenzie almost screamed. "How can they end breakfast without calling us, Jim?"

Erroll answered under his breath. "I don't know Jane, but just in case Dal's around, we don't want to make waves."

"How can we be sure we won't miss breakfast tomorrow, or any other day?"

"Maybe it's not worth a fuss, Jane. Maybe we can take some bread or something to our room each evening, sleep as late as we want, and eat the bread when we want."

Kenzie's face flushed and she raised her voice even more. "Erroll, we paid for that breakfast."

Erroll put his finger on his lips, and answered quietly. "No, Jane, we didn't pay for anything. Somebody did, but not us. Don't talk so loud. Somebody'll hear you."

Kenzie shifted the target of her anger to Erroll. "Do you think I care if somebody hears, or whether we paid or somebody else paid? Our tickets paid for breakfast. We should have it."

Erroll put his finger to his lips again. "It's all right, Jane. Maybe you can get it out of 'em at lunch."

"You don't understand anything, Erroll. Our tickets include breakfast. They have no right to sneak it out and not tell us."

"Let's go back to our room and wait for lunch time."

"You go, Erroll. I intend to give these people a piece of my mind."

"No Jane, you mustn't. We don't want to make waves, remember?"

"*You* don't want to make waves. I'll make as many waves as I want."

"I don't see anybody to insult. Let's go to our room, Jane."

"I'm not going yet. I'm . . . well, if you say we must."

"Thanks, Jane."

The ship remained at the dock and took on freight all day and into the evening; it steamed down the river the next morning. The departure awakened Erroll and Kenzie, but again too late for breakfast.

They arrived at Moville during the night, and stayed there the following day and night. Erroll professed to be certain they wouldn't see Dal again, but Kenzie asserted they would. Bunches of people came on and off the ship during the day after the night docking, and the Patersons watched the to and fro action part of the time. Kenzie grabbed Erroll's arm, in the late afternoon. "Look, Jim. There's Dal's hat."

"Are you sure, Jane?"

"I'm dead sure . . . wait. Well, it's a hat like Dal's, but somebody else is under it."

"I thought so, Jane."

"It doesn't make sense for you to be so complacent. If Dal puts a rifle to your head to shoot you, you won't see him."

"We'll soon know. One of the guys in the lunch line said we leave here in the morning. If we're still aboard then, we'll be on our way for sure."

"As always, I hope you know."

The ship left Moville the next morning, and Kenzie reacted. "Erroll, how did you know? Dal can't catch us now."

"Go ahead and relax, Kenzie. Every time a wave crashes against us you'll be closer to the life you talked about after we left Invergarry."

They spent most of their time below deck, but ventured up on top a few times each day to look at the ocean. Kenzie asked while on the top deck the third day out of Moville, "Do you think we'll be closer to seven days or ten days?"

"Maybe ten. We feel a headwind each time we come up here, and it seems a little stronger every day. I don't know how much difference it makes, but it can't help."

"The ship goes up and down a little, but I'm not seasick, are you?"

"No, I don't think I'm susceptible to that."

"Erroll! How can you know? How many days've you been on an ocean?"

"You're right, I don't know. Maybe you're about to talk me into it. Let's go back to our room."

They returned to their room. The gentle pitch of the ship increased to an uncomfortable level by evening. Erroll admitted, "I don't feel well. I know we missed breakfast again today, but let's skip supper tonight."

"Erroll, I understand, and don't think you should eat if you don't feel like it. But I'm hungry. I think I'll go."

Kenzie returned with news after only a few minutes. "The food people say the sea's too rough for us to keep dishes on a table. They say we're headed into a major squall that will probably last most of the day tomorrow. All they gave us is a thick slice of bread."

The Patersons didn't go up on top the next day, but around noon a soaking wet member of the crew walked by their room, and Kenzie talked to him. "What's it like outside?"

"We got a drivin' rain ma'am. The wind's a blowin' ninety to nuthin'. I'm supposed to say it happens a lot and we ain't in no danger, but I ain't seen a wind like this before. You feelin' all right?"

"Yes, I'm fine. My husband felt seasick yesterday, but strangely enough, he feels a little better today. Neither of us have eaten for almost twenty-four hours though, and that's taking a toll on us."

"Ain't nobody had nuthin' but bread, ma'am. But if we don't break apart, we'll be out o' this tonight or tomorrow, and then we'll all eat our heads off."

The storm didn't let up for the rest of the day, the night, or for a short time into the following day. The ship's up and down motion slackened around midmorning the next day, and seemed completely normal by late afternoon, as did Erroll. The Patersons went up to look, and saw a couple little patches of blue sky. The cafeteria served food at noon that day, and everybody, Erroll included, made up for the lost meals.

During the late morning on the seventh day out from Moville, somebody from the crew knocked on the Paterson's door, and Erroll opened it. The person announced, "We can see New York. You might want to go up on the top deck and watch us into port."

Kenzie spoke in a rush. "Erroll, I dreamed about this day since we bought land in Missouri. I never really thought it would come, but you insisted it would. I intend to kiss you now." Erroll grinned, allowed her to do it, and kissed her back. The ship approached land at a barely perceptible rate, but eventually they saw they were in a bay, and then they headed toward a smaller bay off the bigger one, and could see the Statue of Liberty. Kenzie exclaimed, "Look at that, Erroll! Do you remember seeing that when we left here with Poppa?"

"You mean the Statue of Liberty? No, I don't remember it."

"Me either. It's worth every ounce of struggle we went through just to see it. I'm so proud to be part of the country it represents."

"Right, Kenzie, me too. Maybe I understand why Poppa wanted us to come back. I wish he could see us now."

The ship docked a little before dusk, and the instant their turn came to get off, they did. Erroll looked triumphantly at Kenzie and exclaimed, "We're back, Kenzie! We're back!"

She tightened her grip on Erroll and chortled, "I'm going to kiss you again, Erroll." Kenzie kissed him, and for the first time in his life he failed to react.

Appendix 1

Relevant Names

Anderson, Cecil	US Land Merchant in Scotland
Bradley, James	Brother of Burt Bradley, buggy owner, befriended Erroll and Kenzie Paterson
Bradley, Burt	Husband of Thelma Bradley, befriended Erroll and Kenzie Paterson
Bradley, Thelma	Befriended Erroll and Kenzie Paterson
Butler	Employee of McCarty estate
Cox, Darlene/Ralph	Kenzie Paterson's parents
Tiny Kirk	Church in Inverness
Tiny Kirk Wagon Route	West out of Inverness, across McCarty land, past Beauty Firth, south to Drumnadrochit, then northwest back to Inverness
Herd 1	Beauty Firth Beauties Ron Everett, son of Kalindra, early crew leader Ted, later crew leader Bob and Orville, early crew members Ray replaced Orville later; Bob also moved
on	
Herd 2	Middle Valley Herd Ike McCord, early crew leader George, later crew leader Jimmy and Thomas early crew members

	Jon McCandless replaced Jimmy during first year
Herd 3	The Hummer Bunch Art Alston, early crew leader Thomas, different from the Herd 2 Thomas, a later crew leader Stan and Thomas, early crew members
Liveryman	Employee of McCarty estate
Pastor MacIntire	Tiny Kirk
McCarty, Arthur	Edna's father
McCarty, Dal	Son of the supposed Eric McCarty
McCarty, Edna	Daughter of Arthur McCarty, wife of John Paterson, mother of Erroll Paterson
McCarty, Eric	Edna McCarty's older brother
McDowell, Ed	Grocer in Invermoriston
Oscar	Broke up marriage of Darlene/Ralph Cox
Paterson, Aileen	Mother of John Paterson
Paterson, Erroll	Son of John/Edna Paterson
Paterson, John	Married Edna McCarty, father of Erroll Paterson
Paterson, Kenzie Cox	Daughter of Darlene/Ralph, married Erroll Paterson
Sampson	Employee of McCarty estate
Shier, Cecelia	Missouri land seller
Shier, Ed	Cecelia Shier's deceased husband
Smalley, Rex	Early overseer of Athur McCarty's estate

Appendix 2

Relevant Dates

March 3, 1849	John Paterson's birthday
February 12, 1858	Edna McCarty's birthday
Fall, 1876	Edna McCarty begins at University of Rochester
Spring, 1880	Edna McCarty finishes at University of Rochester
June 1, 1880	Edna McCarty/John Paterson marry
January 12, 1882	Erroll John Paterson's birthday
January 14, 1882	Kenzie Albretta Cox's birthday
January 15, 1882	Edna Paterson dies
February 1, 1883	John Paterson takes informal custody of Kenzie Cox
October 15, 1886	First letter from McCarty estate arrives
April 4, 1887	Patersons leave Rochester on Erie Canal
April 10, 1887	Patersons reach New York City
April 20, 1887	Patersons reach Glasgow
April 23, 1887	Patersons reach McCarty estate
February 15, 1904	John Paterson dies
February 16, 1904	Erroll and Kenzie marry
June 28, 1912	Erroll and Kenzie buy land in Missouri

Appendix 3

Shack to New York Progress

Friday, June 28, 1912	Buy Missouri farm
Saturday, 29	Walk from shack to south edge of Inverness
Sunday, June 30	From Inverness to north of Drumnadrochit
Monday, July 1	From north of Drumnadrochit to Invermoriston
Tuesday, 2	From Invermoriston to south of Fort Augustus
Wednesday, 3	From south of Fort Augustus to Invergarry
Thursday, 4	From Invergarry to woods north of Spean Bridge
Friday, 5	Still in woods north of Spean Bridge
Saturday, 6	From woods to near Spean Bridge
Sunday, July 7	No travel
Monday, 8	Spean Bridge to north of Fort William
Tuesday, 9	North of Fort William to Ben Nevis, also north of Fort William
Wednesday, 10	North of Fort William to Fort William
Thursday, 11	To North Ballachulish
Friday, 12	North side of Loch Leven, east from North Ballachulish
Saturday, 13	To Port Glasgow
Sun, Mon, 14, 15	No travel
Tuesday, 16	Board ship
Saturday, 27	Arrive in New York